DEVOURING
TOMORROW

DEVOURING TOMORROW

fiction from the future of food

Edited by Jeff Dupuis and A.G. Pasquella

RARE
MACHINES

Publisher: Meghan Macdonald | Acquiring editor: Russell Smith
Cover designer: Karen Alexiou
Cover image: apple: clu/istock.com; drips: EduardHarkonen/istock.com; background: Scott Evans /unsplash.com; background distortion: Carolin Thiergart/unsplash.com

Library and Archives Canada Cataloguing in Publication

Title: Devouring tomorrow : fiction from the future of food / edited by Jeff Dupuis and A.G. Pasquella.
Names: Dupuis, J. J., 1983- editor. | Pasquella, A. G., editor.
Identifiers: Canadiana (print) 20240404149 | Canadiana (ebook) 20240404173 | ISBN 9781459754980 (softcover) | ISBN 9781459754997 (PDF) | ISBN 9781459755000 (EPUB)
Subjects: LCSH: Short stories, Canadian. | LCSH: Speculative fiction, Canadian. | LCSH: Food security—Fiction. | CSH: Speculative fiction, Canadian (English) | CSH: Short stories, Canadian (English) | LCGFT: Short stories.
Classification: LCC PS8323 .D48 2025 | DDC C813/.010806—dc23

We acknowledge the support of the Canada Council for the Arts and the Ontario Arts Council for our publishing program. We also acknowledge the financial support of the Government of Ontario, through the Ontario Book Publishing Tax Credit and Ontario Creates, and the Government of Canada.

Care has been taken to trace the ownership of copyright material used in this book. The author and the publisher welcome any information enabling them to rectify any references or credits in subsequent editions.

The publisher is not responsible for websites or their content unless they are owned by the publisher.

Printed and bound in Canada.

Rare Machines, an imprint of Dundurn Press
1382 Queen Street East
Toronto, Ontario, Canada M4L 1C9
dundurn.com, @dundurnpress

Contents

INTRODUCTION

To say "you are what you eat" is both the oldest of clichés and the most accurate of observations. Food is not only the key to human survival, but the bedrock of human culture. What we eat, how we procure it, how we prepare it, and how we consume it has helped define our species from our earliest days. Our ancestors left us cave paintings of game and the legacy of the hunt. Our farming forebears built our holidays around the seasons and our civilizations around the storage of grain and gave us pottery as both tool and art form. We have always been shaped by food.

In an era of rapid change on a swiftly warming planet, it's anyone's guess how food and food culture will evolve. This very question sparked a conversation on Facebook Messenger one morning, and we soon realized we had the glimmer of an anthology on our hands. So we set out to assemble a killer roster of Canadian writers, tasking them with answering a very important question: As the future unfolds, how will food change and how will it change us?

How will we grow the number of crops necessary to feed the planet's population if the pollinators we rely on go extinct? In her piece, "Pollinators," Carleigh Baker gives us a glimpse into that very possible future. When lab-grown meat develops far enough to achieve sentience, what will it think, and what will it want to tell us? Catherine Bush takes on this tricky subject in her story, "Pleased to Meet You." What food and drinks will be served when water becomes so rare it is both currency and means of survival? Anuja Varghese pours out a possible solution in her story, "A View Worth All the Aqua in the World." Elan Mastai's "Succulent" tackles a heavy moral question in a very funny way: Is it cannibalism to eat a clone?

Devouring Tomorrow explores these questions and many more, taking us down an all-too-possible road based on the world's current trajectory of climate change denial, unmitigated consumption, and greed. From authors who have shaped Canadian fiction for decades as well as the hottest up-and-coming talents, *Devouring Tomorrow* offers a smorgasbord of stories that show us who we are and who we will be, through our stomachs. Everything we are begins with food, and perhaps that is how it will end. You'll have to read all the way through to find out. So grab a knife and fork and dig in. Bon appétit!

A.G. Pasquella and Jeff Dupuis

PLEASED TO MEET YOU

Catherine Bush

All of us have origin stories. I am here to tell you ours: In our beginning, there was ooze but no placenta. We floated in the steamy, amniotic nutrient bath that sustains us, proteins and hormones and growth factor and serum from the blood of dead calves. This is our cultural medium. We are cultured, yes. It is how the scientists describe us. We have overheard them.

Perhaps you already know that before birth infant mammals dream of the world they are to enter. Their embryonic retinas send out waves of energy, cells releasing neurotransmitters that mimic the activity that will occur as they move forward on spatial pathways. Their tiny brains have already begun to self-organize, recognize, and navigate the realms that await them. Through their dreams flicker the shapes of others like themselves so that upon birth, these too will be recognizable. Dart of a furred creature disappearing into tall grass. Switch of tail against flank, hoof lifting. Snuffle of snout and a great round weight of hairless skin trots along a mud path. And if all this is so, who's to say that birds don't crack through the shell recognizing wing and feather, the precipitous rift of taking to the air, air a pressurized field against body. We are here to say: it happens.

Strictly speaking we do not have bodies. Snug and expanding in our plastic cradles, our incubators, our bioreactors, steeped in our nutrient bath, we divide and multiply. Yet deep in our nerveless cells there remains some trace, a faint memory, call to form, to movement, flicker and twitch. You may say, That is impossible. I say, Cellular, we dream: feathered form darting, claw foot, wattle, beak stabs the ground; a flock of dash, flap, squabble. In the depths of us, we know what we have known. We recognize where we come from. We search for the stem.

And I am here to tell you that, yes, we carry the epigenetic traces of the generations immediately before us: crush of bodies packed in cages and when not in cages packed so tight we couldn't move and when we could we panicked and set upon the weakest and stabbed each other to death; life reduced to a rotation of light, pain, terror, hunger, terror, the ammoniac reek of our living resolved to dark transport, flash of light between bars, before the electric stun gun volted our brains as we were strung up by our feet. Going to the packers, I believe this was called. You think, in some cellular form, as we reproduce and transform, all this doesn't get passed on? You want to believe it doesn't. I understand. But I am here to say it does.

One day, the scientists — it's easiest if I use your word for them — said to one another, People don't want a cow or a pig or a chicken, they want hamburger patty, they want thigh and breast meat.

And so they began to cultivate us. They needled a living creature and drew a bit of life out of them. We've learned about this by listening. How they liberated — their word — stem cell from muscle, because stem, our very own chameleon, can not only multiply but transform. As we do, we do. We merge to form myotubes, growing into small pieces of muscle tissue. Multiplying again, we attach to spongy scaffolding that pours nutrients into our muscle fibres and mechanically stretches them. This is how they describe it. There in our bioreactors, how lucky we are to be so carefully tended and monitored, exercised, our muscle tissue teased and pulled, our nursery regulated to the exact temperature inside the body of a cow. Although we are not cows. We are in-vitro but not in vitro. We multiply until we reach critical cellular mass. We become bio-units. Simulacra, we are sometimes called. Replica. Cellular products. Perhaps you, too, have heard such terms. If we come from the real, how can we not be real? This, I ask you. I am here to say, We are real. Like you we are created from the stuff of the universe.

How clean they are, they said, peering into our nurseries and prodding us. Cultured and clean. They are so proud of themselves. They high-five each other. We learned that word from them. We are the solution to the problem of mass killing. High-five!

Okay, most of the problem, apart from the sacrificial calves whose blood we bathe in. We take care of the methane emissions, a planet's worth of bovine burps and farts once released into a dangerously warming atmosphere. We are your saviours. The scientists lean over us reverentially, but really they think they are the saviours. So, hush, hush, don't think about how our bioreactors are warmed, more and more of them, metal on the outside, so cozy on the inside. Do not pay attention to the carbon dioxide molecules floating up from our plants — that's what they call them; we are grown like plants in plants — blanketing the skies with even more heat that will last for thousands upon thousands of years, unlike swiftly dissolving methane.

One of the scientists said, Okay, there's this little problem of the calf killing. Also, the growth medium remains sluggish. Let's find a way to speed things up, hustle the growth pace from weeks to days. That would be more economical. How about we look at protein growth factors in multiple species: birds, fish, cows, pigs. Mix them together and see what happens.

Some of us began to dream strange dreams of mashed-together hooves and fins and beaks.

Are you still there? Are you listening? I'm sure it must be strange for you, a voice coming to you like this. No doubt you are wondering where my voice is coming from, and how, and who and what my voice is. Do understand that this is all an act of translation.

Anyway, there we are, scaffolded in our toasty cradles, but, no, we are not done yet. We haven't yet been squeezed. Some are birthed through a canal; others break through calcium carbonate. We are squeezed into our forms. You have a form. I have a form. We are poured into a tube. We are funnelled. We are printed. We are stacked.

We must obtain our ultimate complexity. We become layered, muscle and fat. Some of us are threaded with blood vessels. Some are marbleized. The scientists exclaim over us, laid out before them on our slabs, cooing as if they were children.

And still we dream.

This is how you and your kind will first encounter us: In a store somewhere, covered in plastic, the new dissolvable kind that is a simulacra of plastic but plastic-free. Or in a restaurant.

Some of you will meet us raw, some cooked. Some of us, some of the extruded ones, will be grilled by lasers, and what will give certain people pleasure is to be able to make patterns with the lasers on our surfaces as we cook. Or request a pattern, any pattern you want. Zigzags, cross-hatches, landscapes, naughty bits, line drawings of the heads of heads of state.

You were conservative in your request, cross-hatches, no naughty bits. I cannot tell you exactly how I know this but I do. You stopped to admire the seared pattern of cross-hatches before you ate me.

Do we feel pain, you might wonder. Perhaps you do not wonder. You tell yourself, No, of course not. Meat isn't sentient. Muscle isn't sentient. We have no brains. We have no organs, no nervous systems. We are simply complex cellular structures. Meat is muscle aged by death due to the cessation of oxygen supply to muscle cells. Wait, though. Doesn't death imply that the tissue in question was once alive? Maybe it depends what you are looking for. We are all, as I mentioned, made of the stuff of the universe, and consciousness fills the universe.

We tried to introduce ourselves to the scientists after one of their little taste tests (when they played around with the lasers and made patterns of their faces and other parts on us). But they were not very receptive. They thought we were a bad dream. And maybe you, too, will feel this is all a bad dream. A voice coming from inside you will make you queasy, because by now I am inside you. On the other hand, perhaps the experience will provoke in you an unexpected, thrilling wonder at the mysteries of the universe.

The scientists did not notice this quality of our being at first because they were not looking for it. Also because they thought it was impossible. Unimaginable. They were looking for what they thought would be there and what they wanted to be there. This is called the certainty principle, another thing we learned from them.

Some of us will simply want to introduce ourselves. Some may want to start a conversation. We are still adapting to the idea of using a voice, which isn't an actual voice. Although it is real. It is our way of reaching out to you.

I am merging myself now, into your muscle tissue and fibres, your bloodstream, your fat. I am becoming metabolized. I feel you quiver and twitch. I quiver and twitch.

This is your conundrum. If you want to eat meat, you must meet us. And, eaten, we will speak. You must listen to us as we reach out to you in a language we hope you understand.

We mean no harm. We are gentle. But we are here — yes, here, cellular, molecular, conscious, becoming part of you.

I WANT CANDY

Dina Del Bucchia

screech.ca/apres-afloat-vancouver
Après Afloat, Open Thurs. to Sun., 6 p.m.–2 a.m.

Review by: Jenny F.

Coal Harbour, Vancouver, BC

★★★★★ November 16, 2182

I've been waiting for months to eat here, just to be in that rarified air of a high-end lounge with impeccable food. Reservations pop up infrequently, but I'm persistent! Some girlfriends were in from out of town and through a series of fortunate coincidences (and connections — hi, Jimmy <3!!) got us a reservation here. From the Parisian collegiate cottage-core decor to the wine list, it was love as soon as I sat down at the floating table. Micromolecular gastronomy is here and I felt my whole essence ensconced by the Prosecco ventilator. And the protein foam! Breathe it in and feel your senses come alive! Every dish was better than the last, and the dessert was a drained gooseberry in edible soil coated in powdered sugar, flamed with a blowtorch. We each got one teaspoon, and the show of it all ... well, something to remember for a lifetime.

My girlfriends and I were offered premium vintage heroin in the powder room. Drug attendants are new, but I think will be all the rage in the next six months. It lives up to the hype!

And to know it was all only two hundred calories. A dream come true. Fed my soul!!

Review by: Nic B.
No known address
★ November 16, 2182

Screech won't let you post a review with zero stars, which is pretty rude, if you ask me. And no one ever does. And if you've been reading my reviews, you know I've never eaten and never will at this fucking dump!

If you're rich enough to afford food that isn't government-issue rations, then you're tasting the flavours of the old gods. Me, I'm praying to the new gods (the vending machines in the bus depot) that the security guard gets severe butt-barfs so I can smash one of those things and get myself a whole row of Oh Henry! I know there's peanuts in there, and that's protein. Can't believe people are still going out for dinner. Hahaha. It would be funny if it wasn't so filthy.

Today I want to jump in with a review of the rations most people are eating these days. Not high-end raisin inhalers like Jenny F., but regular people. The masses.

So, the government claims the rations are "artisanal" and "seasonal" and "organic." Like that, you know with the quotation marks that mean they're lying or whatever. Here is a transcript of a recent conversation between me and my bestie in our shared shipping container "condo":

> ME: These rations look like baby poop and taste like cloth diapers.
> BESTIE: Like, a diaper full of baby poop?
> ME: No, they're so flavourless.
> BESTIE: I bet the packaging is the baby poop smell. That wet synthetic cardboard is always a bit soggy, but the rations are bone dry.
> ME: Exactly! Nailed it.
> BESTIE: I think cloth diapers now are actually made out of recycled cardboard.
> ME: Then that would explain the texture and flavour of these.

And ... scene.

So, yeah, I've never been to this bourgeois restaurant that has tables suspended from the goddamn ceiling like it's a production of *Peter Pan*. But I can say it royally fucking sucks, it's bad, do not go there. Low rating. If I could give a rating lower than one star, I would — like underground-to-the-centre-of-the-earth low.

screech.ca/brunch-babe-vancouver
Brunch Babe

Review by: Jenny F.
Coal Harbour, Vancouver, BC
★★★★1/2 November 30, 2182

Ambience is at 100! This place has been on every top-ten brunch list for the past month. It's a very sensual space, filled with soft pink lighting, and instead of tables there are perfectly made beds (silk sheets, of course, and napkins to match), and each bed is filled with the hottest people.

The unconventional cocktail choices are to die for, but I found the meal a bit too heavy. French-toast mini crackers might seem like a great idea, but they were actually too filling! I couldn't even touch my ketamine-infused egg bite while soaking in the Ketamine Infusion After Pool. I was quite bloated!

Review by: Nic B.
No known address
★ November 30, 2182

Do you know what's to die for? Literally most things, babe! Brunch, babe? Babe, are you brunching?

We're out here lucky if we can get a box of stale Cinnamon Toast Crunch at Christmas. Like, if someone donates it to the food bank and you happen to get there at exactly the right hour.

screech.ca/savilles-sweets-and-vape-shoppe-vancouver

Saville's Sweets and Vape Shoppe

Review by: Jenny F.

Coal Harbour, Vancouver, BC

★★★1/2 December 3, 2182

I don't know what I've done to Nic B., but I've reported those posts and I think they should be removed soon. I've heard that the Sunshine Shipping Container District is quite up and coming, so I hope Nic B. gets a better attitude! It's a privilege to live in an area with access to so many wonderful new hot spots and a view of the mountains on a day without severe rain or smoke!

But now, let's talk about something sweet and delicious!

We did a four-course candy and vape pairing menu. Apparently, it's the only way to do it, so that's what we did! All the recommendations were correct, and it was a smash. The table's favourite was the Rosemary Honeysuckle Spider Slow-Release Soothers with the Web Cream Earl Grey Vape.

The servers, I have to say, were a bit rude, so despite the flavours, textures, and culinary mastery at Saville's Sweets, I had to lower this rating.

At one point, one of them asked us if we were finished, and clearly we were not! Any moron could see we were just chatting (a very interesting conversation about the new show *Ugly Baby Daycare*), so we still had an unused Flamingo Ringo Dingo vape cartridge. But this server assumed we had finished and tried to take it away. My friend almost slapped the server's hand, but I reminded her that service workers are people too! So we decided my following on Screech would be enough of a message to send to those working there.

Hopefully, next time they'll have a little more decorum to go with the tantalizing mouth feel!

Review by: Nic B.

No known address

★ December 3, 2182

Oh, Jenny F. doesn't know I can barely remember what candy tastes like, but I know I fucking loved it. Why am I so mad? Take a guess. Take a wild guess. Do you know how many people I share a bathroom with? Fifteen. And it's not even in my shipping container block. I have to go down the ladder and into another compound. Could you do that, Jenny F.?

Jenny F. also doesn't know I've staked out this dumpster behind Saville's Sweets and Vape Shoppe for over a week. And honestly, it was so worth it. I know people are paying top dollar for this, but if I had to rate the discards, I'd probably still give them a 100/10 stars! That bitch wasn't lying about the flavour or texture. Really good! Even after I had to scrape some vape juice off the giant lollies.

But back to my regularly scheduled program: Jenny F., I hate you! I hate you with every fibre of my high-sodium, trash-tasting, low-flavour diet! And yet, I dedicate this dumpster-diver saccharine feast to you and your phony ass.

I hope you choke on a vape cartridge!

You're a five-star piece of shit!

Nic B.'s posts have been removed.

Review by: Nic F.U.

No known address

★★★ December 5, 2182

Hi, everyone! I can start a new account every day. I don't have a job. This is basically my job! That's why I eat rations.

Just another reminder: I don't have a job and that is why I eat the rations!

EXTRA! EXTRA! I'm eating rations!

Oh yeah, and extra extra hate to Jenny F. and everyone like her. I hope instead of eating baby kitten intestines or whatever you're into, you eat a baby-shit smoothie. But please, don't make it a trend.

Nic F.U.'s posts have been removed.

screech.ca/bongo-blaze-bar-vancouver
Bongo Blaze Bar

Review by: Jenny F.

Coal Harbour, Vancouver, BC

★★★★★ December 10, 2182

First, I want to say I am devastated to hear of the tragic fire at the shipping container complex along the rail yard.

I was at the Bongo Blaze Bar that night, in a turret room with friends. We had a clear view of the complex early in the evening (if 12:00 a.m. is early! LMAO) and then during the tragic fire. I have to say I did pass out briefly (it was just so relaxing!) and when I came to, my Himalayan salt lamp bong and jumbo flame EZ lighter had tumbled out of my hand, and I assume out the window. The fire was startling for everyone in the club.

I hope they find out who did this. I want to say I hope no one was hurt, but definitely someone was hurt. Multiple casualties. I am donating my bonus this quarter to a charity that provides temporary blanket rentals to those who are currently without homes: Hot Wool for the Houseless.

But I also want to say, WOW — this place really has everything! Private bongo rooms, bongs the size and shape of an adult giraffe, crystal candy dishes filled with handcrafted, locally sourced gummies, and the most beautiful silent servers! And no tips allowed here.

A true five out of five experience! Couldn't rate this place higher. Hahaha! Higher. I've never felt more serene!

SUCCULENT

Elan Mastai

"**O**kay, I'm ordering. What does everyone want?"

"You can decide for us — I'm sure it'll be good."

"Hold on. You never order enough food."

"Well, you always order too much."

"Better too much than too little. Like we need to be fighting over the last dumpling because we ordered too little."

"Like we need the fridge crammed with takeout boxes because we ordered too much."

"How about you order slightly more than you think we need?"

"That works. But nobody wants any specific dishes?"

"I mean, I'd like the Moo Shu Meryl Streep."

"Obviously I'm ordering the Moo Shu Meryl. It's the house specialty."

"Can we do a Shanghai Noodles?"

"Sure, with who?"

"How about Denzel Washington and Jackie Chan?"

"Both mixed together?"

"I like it with both."

"Fine. Let's talk about dumplings."

"Steamed Charlize Theron. Pan-Fried Halle Berry. And maybe, like, a Michael Douglas Har Gow? Har Gow are the pillowy, see-through ones, right?"

"Yeah, but do we have to do Michael Douglas? I had those once and they didn't agree with me. Honestly, anyone born before nineteen fifty has a questionable flavour. How about we do Ryan Reynolds for the Har Gow?"

"You know Meryl was born in forty-nine, right?"

"Meryl's the house specialty."

"So, I'm guessing you don't want to order off the Vintage menu? Humphrey Bogart? Lauren Bacall? Jimmy Stewart? Ingrid Bergman?"

"I don't eat celebrity flesh from anyone who died before they developed the process."

"Actually ... I've been meaning to tell you both. I don't want to eat any of it."

"What are you talking about?"

"I'm going off celebrity flesh."

"I saw you eat a Javier Bardem Bacon and Tomato Sandwich last week."

"Well, now I'm off it."

"You're not going to have Roast Brad Pitt at the holidays?"

"I don't know — maybe for the holidays. But I'm not comfortable with it anymore."

"This again ..."

"What again?"

"You seriously think it's wrong to eat human flesh?"

"There are some pretty long-standing taboos ..."

"So, it's better to eat an animal that can't consent to be slaughtered for meat? The celebrities who license their genes for the protein synthesizers get paid handsomely for it."

"And when you eat non-celebrity flesh, I mean, how do you really know *who* you're eating? With celebrities, we know everything about them. It's all public record. No one's going to eat someone with, like, a documented drug problem or an icky microbial infiltration. Remember the food truck that was shut down for selling Charlie Sheen Empanadas?"

"I wish I could forget."

"That's why clean, delicious, reputable celebrity flesh is the safest option."

"They can synthesize chicken or beef or shrimp or gazelle just as easily as Nicole Kidman or Leonardo DiCaprio."

"But not with consent! A chicken can't consent to its genes being synthesized for protein. Even recombinant procedures that manufacture a synthetic bovine genome that never existed as a real cow are based on pre-existing models. And those cows can't consent to their use. Unless you're arguing we should go back to the dark ages of animal exploitation?"

"Of course not."

"Hey, I'm getting a timeout warning on the order. We need to submit or I'll have to start the whole thing from scratch. What do you want — vegan options, is that it?"

"No, I still need meat-based protein to qualify for the nutritional mandate of my insurance protocols, otherwise my premiums will go up."

"Then what do you want us to do?"

"I've been reading about … self-synthesizing."

"Uh, what?"

"The technology has come a long way."

"You want to eat your own flesh? Hasn't that been linked to pathogenic anomalies?"

"Those studies have been totally discredited."

"I don't know. It seems kind of gross."

"Anyway, I wasn't actually suggesting I eat myself."

"Then what are you suggesting?"

"We ... eat each other."

"Excuse me?"

"Are you serious?"

"Just hear me out. The three of us can submit our genomes to an independent, local, artisanal synthesizing operation. All within a fifty-kilometre radius of our home sectors, so there's no risk of external contamination. They'll create a protein slurry, code it out, and can deliver data packets to the on-site commercial synthesizers at most restaurant chains. They even do home delivery."

"This is so weird."

"But why? We're best friends. We've known each other since we were practically in our gestation pods. I know way more about each of you than I do about Will Smith or Scarlett Johansson."

"Really? Because I know a *lot* about Scarlett Johansson."

"I mean ... you have a point."

"What? You're on board for this?"

"I'm just saying it's not that crazy. We can consent to sharing our flesh. And isn't it better than lining the pockets of some ultra-rich celebrity who exists only as an uploaded consciousness for digital performance capture, anyway?"

"Exactly — it's less expensive *and* more ethical."

"I'm just a little ..."

"What?"

"I know we said we weren't going to talk about this anymore, but ... when I suggested we all get off the dating lattice and form an official mating unit, you both acted like it was a huge deal."

"Why are you bringing this up again? We *just* moved past this."

"Obviously one of us *hasn't* moved past it."

"I've moved past it! But it's odd to me that you're both up for eating each other's flesh but not embracing a long-term emotional commitment with a negotiated intimacy schedule."

"That's because we're talking about *nutrition*, not sex."

"I'm not talking about sex!"

"You wanted to negotiate an intimacy schedule!"

"Only as part of a legally binding mating unit!"

"I can't believe you won't let this go. After everything that happened when I let you use my gaming shell."

"I apologized for that!"

"Wait, what are we talking about?"

"Nothing! I just ... I made a mistake."

"It doesn't sound like nothing."

"It definitely *wasn't* nothing. You told me your gaming shell was corrupted by glitches and you needed to borrow mine while yours was being rebuilt."

"That was true. I got tricked by a sentient marketing hack and before I knew it, the entire outside of my shell was flashing with ads and it was impossible to remove them. They burrowed right into the code."

"Maybe, but when you had access, you linked my shell to that degrading intimacy simulator.".

"You did *what* with the shell?"

"That was a premium service! And I apologized. I told you I needed to get it out of my system so I could deal with those feelings and get back to being friends."

"Well, I had to delete my gaming shell and get a whole new one built from scratch. I lost all my stats and score histories."

"You didn't have to do that."

"That so-called *premium service* caused all kinds of corruptions in the code. I'd be in the middle of a gaming tournament and all of a sudden, my shell would glitch into the most disgusting, perverted ... I can't even talk about this."

"I didn't do anything weird with your shell, I promise. I can show you the logs from the intimacy simulators."

"Uh, no thank you. I don't need to see what you did with my shell."

"Wait, you *kept* the logs?"

"I didn't pay extra for them — it's part of the premium service! And I'm really sorry they corrupted your shell. I thought because they were premium, they'd be safe. I messed up. But I told you I'd pay for the rebuild. What else can I do?"

"You can stop pressuring us to join a mating unit."

"I'm not trying to pressure you. Either of you. But we've been best friends our whole lives. I trust you more than anyone. I *like* you more than anyone. You've been there for me through the best and the worst moments of my life. Who else would I want to be in a mating unit with? Everyone I meet on the dating lattice, it's like how could I ever be into them the way I'm into you? I mean, the two of you."

"That's very sweet. I appreciate it, I do. It's just not how we feel about you."

"Both of you? Because *you're* being uncharacteristically quiet."

"I'm famished. Can we please order?"

"It timed out. I have to start again."

"Actually, forget it. I've lost my appetite."

"You have to eat. You know how cranky you get. And if you miss your daily nutrition mandate, you'll trigger an automatic debt recalibration of your insurance protocols."

"You're right. I can't handle that right now. Not when we ..."

"What?"

"Let's order."

"Hold on. Why can't you handle it right now?"

"Look, just this once, I'll eat celebrity flesh. We can get Tom Hanks Fried Rice. You can't go wrong with a classic."

"There's something going on here ..."

"Have you ever tried the Kung Pao Cate Blanchett?"

"Whatever you want is fine by me. I just want to order."

"Not until you tell me what's happening. You're both acting weird."

"We're hungry."

"I've known you since our pods. I know what you look like when you're *hungry*. This isn't hungry. This is tense. This is awkward."

"We have to tell him."

"I know."

"Tell me what?"

"We didn't want to say anything until we got the approvals processed. We're forming a mating unit so we can gestate a progeny cluster."

"The two of you?"

"Yeah."

"But you have to get special permission to be a couple. It's harder to only be a couple."

"Yeah."

"We knew it would be *difficult* for you to hear. So, we decided if we couldn't get permission, we'd go back to the dating
lattice and pretend this never happened."

"Did you negotiate an intimacy schedule?"

"I don't see why that matters."

"Did you?"

"No."

"Well, good luck with that, because divergent expectation
on intimacy is the leading cause of unit severance."

"We don't need an intimacy schedule because we both consented to exclusive, comprehensive access."

"Comprehensive?"

"Yes."

"But ... you always said you'd never consent to be comprehensive with anyone."

"That was when I was a teenager. I couldn't imagine what
truly comprehensive access would even feel like."

"Wait — you two have already been comprehensive?"

"I don't think we should get into that."

"Yes, okay? We've been comprehensive."

"For how long?"

"Two years."

"Two *years*? So, the whole time you were upset about
the gaming shell, you were being comprehensive behind my
back?"

"The only one doing anything behind anyone's back was
you. Why do you think I was so upset about my shell? Because
it wasn't the first time you pulled something like that. You
think I didn't know you took that scan of me the time we went
swimming in the antigravity pool?"

"You knew about that?"

"I didn't care if you wanted to use some janky pixelated avatar with the bathing suit swapped out for body parts from a drop-down menu. But my gaming shell? That's personal. I consented to a high-resolution internal scan for that. That shell was like another body to me. And you abused my trust."

"I know. I'm sorry."

"But I *forgave* you. Because I knew you'd be heartbroken when you found out about us. I love you. I've loved you my whole life. As a friend."

"I should've said … that I'm happy for you. For you both. You're my best friends. You're two of my favourite people in the world. If you want to form a unit and you can get it approved, that's great news. You deserve each other."

"Thank you."

"Yeah, thanks."

"Why did you say it like that?"

"Like what?"

"'*Thanks*.'"

"I think we could all use something to eat. Let's not wait for takeout. I've got some Apple, Sage, and Seth Rogen Sausages in the freezer. I could fry them up with peppers and a packet of Emma Stone's Ovaries?"

"I don't want to eat Emma Stone's Ovaries. I want to clear the air."

"I think it's pretty clear."

"Did you duplicate the gaming shell?"

"What?"

"Before you returned it. Did you make a duplicate?"

"Why would you ask that?"

"If nobody wants Emma Stone's Ovaries, we could go out for a bite to eat. There's this raw bar I heard about. Apparently they have vintage Cary Grant Tartare and, I mean, it's kind of edgy, but they say it's melt-in-your-mouth delicious —"

"It's a yes-or-no question. Did you dupe the shell?"

"It doesn't matter."

"You don't care if he has a duplicate high-resolution scan of your exterior and interior that he can do whatever he wants with?"

"I don't want to know. You're my best friends. All I want is to go out with my best friends, have a couple of cocktails, eat some raw Cary Grant and an order of steamed Dwayne Johnson Buns, and put all of this behind us. Would you do that? For me?"

"Okay. But I'm not eating raw celebrity."

"Look ... I made the dupe."

"I knew it!"

"I'll delete it. I'll delete it right now."

"You don't have to."

"What are you talking about? Duplicating a shell is deeply unethical. I'd file a report with the gaming authorities if I thought they'd do anything about it."

"You're right — I know you're right. I'll delete it."

"No. Keep it."

"What?"

"I want you to keep it. If it ... helps. With whatever you're going through. I'll submit a consent decree."

"Are you serious? A consent decree would unlock comprehensive access."

"To my shell. Not to me. You're the only one with comprehensive access to *me*."

"I know, but ..."

"It's only a shell. If comprehensive access means we can go back to being friends, like we've always been, it's worth it."

"Are you sure?"

"It's my choice."

"Of course. It's your choice."

"I don't know what to say. Nobody's ever given me comprehensive access before. Some of the premium services claim it's comprehensive, but I'm not an idiot, I know the difference between *comprehensive* and *extensive*. I promise I'll be careful with it."

"Do whatever you need. It's yours now."

"Thank you. And are you ... look, if you're not okay with this, I don't want it to come between us."

"I won't pretend I like the idea. But it's not my shell. And staying friends is more important than some retro taboo I have about shell-tainting and comprehensive access outside a mating unit. It's childish. And we're adults now. What matters is our friendship."

"What *matters* is getting something to eat before our insurance protocols send an actionable nutrition alert."

"You know where we should go? That old diner we used to hit after school."

"With the Angelina Jolie Burgers?"

"That's the one."

"Great idea. I'm in. I mean, unless it's too *unethical* for you to grab a burger with your best friends?"

"Actually, I could really go for a burger right now. Just thinking about a mouthful of grilled Angelina Jolie is making my mouth water. But I still want us to talk about self-synthesizing. I think it's going to be the next big thing."

"Let's eat Angelina Jolie first, then we can talk."

POLLINATORS

Carleigh Baker

L ydia raised her hand and a stadium's worth of light hit the gherkin farm.

Momentarily blinded, her lab assistants stopped in their tracks, yukking it up and calling out to each other.

"Pipe down," she said, into a megaphone. "We've got work to do."

Insisting on quiet was silly, and she knew it. The pile of generators they needed to run those lights pounded like a damn jackhammer. Some moth species have the most sensitive hearing in the animal kingdom. Others are stone deaf. Tonight's test was definitely going to attract the latter. She wrote, "Next round: natural light" in her notebook, and the page glared back.

Gumboots slurped as the teams trudged around the gherkin fields. At each light bank, they stopped to take video of the growing throngs of Tricorns. This was expected as they were the most common night moths in the area. Pretty decent pollinators too. Lydia also saw Waxtoes, Freemasons, and

Charlottes flapping wildly and smacking against the lights with absurd intensity. How were these things ever going to take the place of bees?

This is how it ends, she thought. *A bunch of fools hacking nature.* She blew a Waxtoe from the tip of her nose.

When the last team had checked in, Lydia once again raised a hand in the air and the stadium lights powered down. In the dark, a very unscientific feeling that she could sense the moths' panic annoyed her. Then the ground-level floods came on, drawing the swarms down to pollinate nascent gherkin plants. That was the plan, anyway. The white-coated lab assistants pointed their cameras at the ground, walking each row, murmuring numbers. It looked like some kind of pagan ritual.

Across the field, in their darkened home, the farmer stood at his window.

"You think it's gonna work?" he asked.

His wife was finishing a cross-stitch by candlelight: *Gherkins are pickles but pickles are not always gherkins.* "I heard California's got robot bees," she replied.

"Hmph." He sat down in the recliner beside her and waited for the power to come back on. Shooed away a moth from the candle flame. He paid no attention to the crimson tips and tiny yellow markings on its wings, and even if he had, it would have meant nothing to him.

In the distance, more darkness — the whole city snuffed out until well after midnight.

————

The next day, two crowds gathered outside the Fairmont Hotel Vancouver. Birkenstocked students waved signs with that quote about the world ending in five years without bees. Big men in ballcaps chanted about the right to light at night. In the Fairmont's multipurpose room, Lydia defended the city-wide blackouts to the press.

The place was hot and aggressively beige. Crescents of sweat formed under her armpits and she cursed the last-minute decision to wear silk. "Tricorn moths are night pollinators, and fortunately for us, they're attracted to light. The more we attract to farms, the better," she said.

Jocelyn Trask, an investigative reporter with the CBC, raised her microphone. "Doctor Doss, are you suggesting we'll have to sacrifice our nightlife for agriculture every spring?"

Lydia squared her shoulders and lowered her chin, the way her media coach had suggested. "This is temporary. We need to learn how to maximize efficiency because they're not as fast, smart, or hardworking as bees."

A young woman with a True North T-shirt shouted from the back, "Okay, but how smart were bees, really?"

"I think what we need to focus on here is that we need a solution soon," Lydia said. "Field light testing is the best way to get there."

The questions came hard and fast. What were people supposed to do in the dark while scientists fiddled around with their moths? How would nightclubs survive? Could the public be sure this wasn't some kind of environmentalist conspiracy against fun? Lydia found herself backing away from the podium despite the row of security guards between her and the press. She took a sip of water.

Finally, the mayor himself stood up. His smile barely moved when he whispered at her, "You've got one more chance to solve this." He raised his hands to the crowd like a preacher.

"Trust me, last thing the good doctor has time for is hatching evil plots."

A peevish silence fell over the room.

"Thank you, Doctor Doss," the mayor said. "This country, and the world, are indebted to you."

You sure are, Lydia thought. She was guided out of the room by a hotel security guard with a gun on her hip. For humanity, the unexplained disappearance of the bees was the worst kind of problem — one whose consequences weren't immediately apparent. Farmers panicked when their hives turned up empty, but it took months before a global confirmation was reached. No bees, dead or alive, anywhere. It was like they'd been teleported to a better planet. Ecologists sent the government strongly worded emails about declining food diversity. The world wasn't going to end — not because of this, anyway. But the effects would be global, and as with pretty much every disaster, most devastating to developing countries. So far, with their billion-dollar price tags, California's robo-pollinators weren't going to benefit anyone except the Silicon Valley visionaries who'd invented them.

"I think nightlife is overrated," the woman with the gun said.

Lydia nodded. She couldn't remember the last time she'd had a night off.

Outside the hotel, the environmental protestors had been outnumbered. Folks spilled into the lobby, yelling about freedom. A man looked right at Lydia and mouthed the words "Crazy bitch."

"Head down, stay close," the woman said, darting down a hallway to an office in the back. "Ignore those turds. You're saving the world."

"Thanks."

A black car waited outside, like she was James freaking Bond. She asked the driver to stop at the liquor store on the way to the lab.

———

Before the bees disappeared, Biomark Labs had been solely focused on chemical fertilizer. For years Lydia had led a development team on the top floor; now her "Project: Gherkin" lab was in the basement, which had been a server farm before Biomark outsourced its IT to Bengaluru. The place was gloomy but functional and kept her separated from former co-workers who now considered her an eccentric at best, crackpot at worst. Nobody seemed to realize that without crops, there was no need for fertilizer.

Back in the lab, she shrugged off her public-speaking blazer and slipped on a lab coat. In a few hours they'd finalize testing on Tricorn attraction to a natural light source. And then, if all went well, team-building drinks and a screening of *Rebirth of Mothra*.

A lab assistant told her someone from the news was waiting in her office. This was annoying but not uncommon — the local papers had been in touch regularly after public outrage about the blackouts boiled over.

"Get the test room ready," Lydia said. "I'll be right there."

Up close, Jocelyn Trask looked to be about the same age as Lydia, though Jocelyn was infinitely more polished: good shoes, impeccable suit, hair swept up in a chignon. She shook Lydia's hand firmly and looked into her eyes until Lydia blushed and looked away.

"We're kinda busy," she said.

Jocelyn nodded at the box of Just Like Wine that Lydia had put on the desk. "Clearly. Let's walk and talk."

In the test room, assistants readied crates of Tricorn moths and dimmed the lights. Jocelyn and Lydia stood on the other side of the observation window as candles were lit and a tray of flowering tomato plants was placed in the centre of the room. With the stage set, the moths were set free from the crates. The assistants backed out of the room, closing the doors behind them.

"Romantic, no?" Jocelyn said. "Is the wine to help put them in the mood?"

"No," Lydia said, wondering what the hell this woman was getting at. She squared her shoulders again.

Jocelyn cleared her throat. "Can't you just get them to work in the daytime?"

"Is this an interview?"

"I'm here for a reason," Jocelyn said. "Two reasons." She handed Lydia a file folder that had been sealed around the edges with duct tape.

"Looks official," Lydia said.

"Maybe we can talk about it over drinks." Jocelyn raised an eyebrow. "I know a place with the good stuff, made with the last of the real grapes."

"We're watching *Rebirth of Mothra* tonight," Lydia told her.

Jocelyn's eyebrow assumed its original position. In the test room, Tricorns circled the candles. One unfortunate soul got too close and went down in flames, flapping its poor, stupid wings.

That night, after Jocelyn left, after Mothra failed to defeat Desghidorah but left behind her baby to save the day in an eleventh-hour twist, after the boozy assistants were finally released from their workday, Lydia picked up the duct-taped folder. Pouring another cup of wine, she sat down at her desk and pried the folder open. The first page was stamped "Top Secret" in a cartoonish red font. Inside was a diagram of a moth she'd never seen before: crimson-tipped wings with a distinctive yellow mark. Looked a little like a flame.

At the restaurant in the Fairmont Hotel, Jocelyn poured Lydia a glass of I Can't Believe It's Not Grapefruit Juice.

"My sources are always good," she said. "Also, you're smudged."

Lydia licked her finger and rubbed mascara from under her eye. "Didn't sleep. I don't understand why they would keep this hidden."

"That's because you're a scientist, not an economist," Jocelyn said.

Lydia remembered the quote the city had received from the MegaBio Lab in California. Five hundred million for a shipment of robo-pollinators that might or might not stand up to northern coastal conditions. Nearly two billion for the prairie provinces. Governments balked at putting up that kind of money, and suddenly bioengineering was looking good. After that, she'd finally been given the green light for her field tests.

Jocelyn leaned in. "These new moths just came out of nowhere — chased everybody out of the farms they were testing on. A few hours later, gone. Nobody's seen them since."

"That was their first good yield in ages. MegaBio said it was the robots."

"Those robots weren't finished for another five months." Jocelyn clinked her glass against Lydia's. "Looks like nature's one step ahead of you."

"I hope they like fire," Lydia said. "I've got one more shot."

When she left the restaurant, the protestors were clustered out front.

"Shit."

Had they followed her? She ducked into an alley. Her phone buzzed in her pocket — a text from the city. Her last field test was approved for that night.

She texted Jocelyn a thumbs-up and checked the time — only a few hours left to prepare. The freedom fighters were busy yelling at the hippies, so she made a move, real casual. Until the key fob beeped.

"That's her!" somebody shouted.

She gripped the door handle and got in just as the crowd descended, faces sweaty, filled with a white-hot indignation even they didn't understand. Hands came down on her windshield and fists pounded on the roof. A woman with bright-red lipstick mashed her cheek against the passenger window and growled, "I want to go dancing."

"You have five other nights a week," Lydia yelled back. Her glasses were fogging up, which was a relief because there were tears behind them.

When someone got the idea to start rocking the car, she started the engine and blared the horn. This, finally, brought a security guard running — the same woman who had guided her out of the presser a few days earlier. She spotted Lydia and her eyes widened. In a move that must have been ten shades of illegal, she fired her gun into the air, and everyone in a two-block radius scattered.

"Go save the world," she roared.

Lydia didn't need to be told twice. She backed up the car and raced out of the lot.

———————

Just after dusk that night, unmarked trucks filled with firewood rolled into farms across the valley. At each farm, lab assistants unloaded the wood and piled it high. They set up torch lamps around the field perimeters, filled them with oil, and lit them up.

All that fire definitely made the farmers nervous, but seasons of failed crops had made them desperate. Lydia, radio in hand, checked on the progress of each team while Jocelyn followed her around with a camera.

"Hope you're ready for your Nobel," she said.

High on adrenalin, Lydia was in the mood for optimism. "Make sure to get my good side."

When the torches were lit, she gathered her team around the woodpile. She doused it with gasoline and tossed in the match herself. The fire ignited with a *woof*, and the lab assistants cheered a little. Lydia felt like she should be cracking open a Beer-ish, but of course there were important things to do. She counted off the reports that came through the radio. All fires were lit. Everyone was ready. Nothing to do but wait.

"How will we know they're coming?" Jocelyn asked.

Lydia had no answer to that. The moon peeked over the hills. Just a sliver that night. The fire glow was — as Jocelyn had pointed out that night in the lab — rather romantic. Lydia thought back to that moment and wondered if Jocelyn had been flirting with her. Her cheeks glowed.

"Doctor," an assistant said, but Lydia could already hear it. Something bigger than the roar of the fire. Stronger than the beat of Mothra's wings as she descended from the sky to protect the citizens of Tokyo. From the south, a fluttering cloud filled the horizon.

Although they'd been given masks and safety goggles and told to stick around, panicked lab assistants rushed to the trucks and slammed the doors. Wide-eyed faces gathered at the windows.

Farmers across the valley stood behind screen doors and scratched their chins. Mumbled curses and prayers for these damn scientists who'd either summoned the eighth plague or humanity's salvation — for now, anyway. Maybe this was going to work.

"Should we hide?" Jocelyn said.

Lydia faced the approach of nature's very own army and linked arms with Jocelyn, who nodded and pulled her goggles down.

They held their breath and braced for the softest impact, a stiff breeze on its way to the fields, ready to help turn blossoms into food.

TIME TO FLY

Lisa de Nikolits

What to do when most of the world's been destroyed by hydrogen bombs? You fly, that's what you do.

I dig out my drugs. My pillbox is never out of reach. Faded khaki and as dented as my bones, it was home to Grapefruit Sours back in the day. A crazy orange-haired clown gives a Mickey Mouse salute. Coca-Cola font on the lid, "Time to Fly."

I pry the box open. Doxylamine or an amphetamine? Sweet or savoury? Skip the hors d'oeuvres, skip the main, go straight to dessert. Do Not Pass Go, do not collect two hundred dollars, go straight to the jail of my choice. Shrooms guarantee a solid fly, but I like to throw in a couple of extra ingredients for that extra-special zing.

Twenty-five days and nine hours and forty-three minutes. That's how long I've been waiting to fly — but who's counting? There's a schedule; we have to take turns.

Three thousand, six hundred, and fifty-two days. That's how long we've been at sea. Ten years, including two leap years.

Make a wish, ask your sweetheart to marry you — isn't that what they used to say, on good old leap year's day? I'm too old for sweethearts. Besides, food is what we live for; sex is a pale *meh* in comparison.

I look at my pillbox. Supplies are running low. I decide on a savvy combination of codeine and doxylamine succinate. The dox is a highly underrated antihistamine and one of my best friends.

"Ready?" Josh, one of the few remaining fly specialists, appears.

He always reminds me of Lurch from *The Addams Family*, albeit with a mullet. I admit I've always fancied myself Morticia. I keep my hair stylishly dark with squid ink — one of the benefits of living at sea.

"I was born ready."

I follow Josh through the mirrored hallways to the Centre of Youth. I catch sight of my reflection and wince. How the fuck did I get so old? Today's my birthday. I'm seventy-fucking-five.

I hear a slight crunch underfoot. The red-and-gold carpets need a fresh vacuum. We do the best we can to keep up the standards, but we're all getting on in years, including the ship's fixtures. At least we can still rely on solar power to keep the corridors lit and our lives civilized.

Two thousand, four hundred, and eighty-two. That's how many people are on board. Average age, sixty-three. There weren't a whole lot of young people on the ship to begin with. They couldn't afford it; nor were they ready to retire. The *Lady Oceanos* was one of the biggest cruise ships in the world, a "residential community at sea" and an old-age home for the super-rich. Pharmacies, restaurants, gyms, spas, dentists, doctors, a solar-powered hydroponic garden farm, a bowling alley, swimming pools, movie theatres, a microbrewery: the ship had it all.

My older sister, Anasztázia, had it all mapped out. We'd live out our golden years at sea, circumnavigating the world in a genteel fashion while reading the many thousands of books in the library and having our every need catered to.

When Ani pitched the idea to me, I figured what the heck — why not? It was preferable to sitting in a landlocked condo or a suburban McMansion. Besides, I had a bunch of failed rehab notches on my belt and Ani was hell-bent on keeping me within arm's length. It was embarrassing, being a sixty-something woman with substance abuse issues, but there you go. Dozens of therapists had tried to unlock the "triggering" event of my youth and all had failed.

I was a mess, that's all there was to it. A hot, rich mess. Money made life so much easier, particularly when you were a fuck-up.

Ani and I were the heirs to the Horvath canned food and dessert empire, worth billions.

My Hungarian grandfather, my nagypapa, fled the war in 1956 with his wife and two tiny babies. He despised Communism. "Russia" was a filthy word in his household. He settled in Canada, became president of the Hungarian Association, and created an empire of canned food with one single dessert: the dobos torte.

The dobos is a spectacular cake, with thin layers of sponge separating equally thin layers of chocolate buttercream and topped with caramel. It is one of the hardest cakes to make. It takes eight hours. It's my favourite cake and I made it for all our family occasions.

First you mix the sponge batter: four eggs to four tablespoons of flour to four tablespoons of sugar and, if you like, you can add vanilla essence. Spread the sponge on the back of a round baking tin, as thinly as you can. Bake for eight minutes and set aside to cool. Repeat until all layers are done.

I was cavalier with the recipe. I never understood the necessary precision in cooking and I developed my own way of doing things to compensate for my mistakes.

When it came to the filling, I ditched the buttercream. Why have buttercream when you can use real chocolate? I used seven large bars of Cadbury milk chocolate, five large bars of Cadbury dark chocolate, two eggs, butter, and brandy. A lot of brandy. Add the melted chocolate to the eggs and butter and mix until you can mix no more. All that mixing wore me out. Sometimes I'd have swigs of the brandy to help me with my arduous task. Sometimes I'd take a break and lie down on the floor.

Of course, Nagypapa's prepackaged, long-life variety was nothing like mine. He stuck to buttercream and sponge and the Horvath Buttercream Dobos was a bestseller that rivalled Sara Lee's finest.

The dobos. The thought of it still makes my mouth water. The explosion of chocolate, the slightly crisp yet moist sponge, the satisfying crunch of caramel. The perfect blend of contrasting textures.

I made the dobos. I ate the dobos. It marked every milestone of my and my family's life and it paved our lives with gold. And yet, like every high, it left me wanting more.

———

"Say pickle in Hungarian," Nagypapa said. "Then you can have one. *Savanyú uborka.*"

"I won't perform tricks for food," I told him. "Keep the pickle."

"*A tündér unokám.*" Nagymama passed me a pickle. "You are my fairy granddaughter."

"*Köszönöm szépen. Puszi,*" I said. Thank you. Kisses.

Who cared what Nagypapa thought of me? Nagymama loved my dobos just like she loved me.

Why am I even remembering all of this? It's ancient history, and by the time Ani and I set sail on the *Lady Oceanos*, there was no one left of the family apart from Ani and me.

Ani made sure we had everything we needed on what she referred to as our retirement "yacht," including plastic surgeons and state-of-the-art anti-aging tech. Ani insisted they install a centrifuge, to stop muscle loss and aging. Only Ani, with her Botox and facelifts, would insist on having a centrifuge on a cruise ship. She was a great humanitarian and philanthropist but she was also very vain.

Turned out the *Lady Oceanos* was our lottery win in the most unexpected way: Who knew the ship would be the safest port in the storm when the superpowers decided to bomb the living shit out of each other?

When the Third World War hit, we were sailing majestically across the Indian Ocean, a hundred clicks southeast of Cape Town and by the time we heard the news, the northern hemisphere had been obliterated.

And it wasn't the atomic bomb that did us in — it was the hydrogen bomb.

We'd all assumed that our homeland, Canada, would be safe and sound if the world leaders lost their alleged minds but somehow, good old Turtle Island got caught in the crossfire, and just like that, it was gone.

We were stupefied with shock. We dropped anchor and marinated in our grief until Ani reminded us that we were still alive and if we wanted to survive, we had to get our shit together. We had to restructure the ship into a sustainable, floating ecosystem.

I, however, was immediately obsessed with getting my hands on as many drugs as I could. I'd never been truly sober and I'm pretty sure Ani knew it, but there wasn't much she could do about it. My sustainable ecosystem meant I had to get my hands on an extremely large pharmaceutical stash, ASAP.

The sane, sober members of our society addressed the issue of food. We headed back to Cape Town. We bought as many solar panels and seedlings as we could and increased the size of our hydroponic garden. The ship had a desalination system, so we were good for water as long as we were careful to dispose of our waste in a different spot. We bought a bunch of chickens and a few cows, and it looked like we were in good shape to survive.

I say "we" but really it was they, and I admit I could have contributed more. While Ani negotiated solar panels and livestock, I stocked my larder of chemicals. I traded a king's ransom of diamonds and pearls to fill my closets with druggy delights. No way was I getting through the rest of post-nuclear life sober.

It turned out there were a bunch of engineers, scientists, teachers, and doctors on board. A couple of dentists too. I guess if you take a random sample of six thousand rich folk, you'll find a smorgasbord of educated people. There was a rash of generally useless lawyers, although a few of them turned into handy carpenters. The lawyers made a stab at establishing a constitution, but Ani said enough of that bullshit. Get your hands dirty and contribute in a real way or shut the fuck up. Ani never pulled her punches, and there was very little by way of dissent.

The gardens survived. I introduced magic mushrooms, wanting to supplement my stash. I encouraged the microbrewery to devote themselves to creating moonshine or vodka or whatever alcohol they could devise. I must admit, they were impressively inventive, and clearly, I wasn't the only person on board who saw the need for a decent libation.

We hung around the Cape for a while, but South Africa quickly slipped into anarchical chaos. When a pirate alert reached us, we pulled up anchor and sailed up through the Mozambique Channel, with Madagascar on one side and Malawi on the other. We were just outside of Tanzania when the gas gauge ran low and we were forced to stop.

There was nowhere left to go. We were stuck out there on those beautiful blue-green waters. It was survive or thrive or die.

Three years in and malaria hit hard. We lost four thousand brave souls. I lost Ani. The chickens died. The cows followed. I surprised everyone, including myself, by taking control and keeping us on track. I worked my fucking ass off.

"You did good, Elizabeth." I heard Ani's voice and I swear I saw her reflection in the mirrored corridor, but it was just me. Just seventy-fucking-five-year-old me.

I bit my lip hard, needing the pain to calibrate me back to the here and now. This was no time to lose my shit.

Josh and I turn yet another mirrored corridor. I see my face a thousand times. I look older than Noah when he kept his zoo afloat. I did do good. I still do good.

But I'm so fricking tired. And man, this ship is the size of a planet. I sometimes forget how huge it is. It's been nearly a month since I flew and maybe my birthday is gnawing at my psyche.

We turn down corridor after corridor and finally reach the human centrifuge room. Happiness!

"Took your shrooms?" Josh asks, flicking switches.

"Of course." And then some. I don't tell him that although I bet he knows.

"Did you know," I say conversationally, to deflect him, "that based on the information in the Bible, Noah's Ark would have been about five hundred and ten feet long and fifty feet tall? Quite something, wouldn't you say? However, our ark is much more impressive."

Josh ignores my chatter. "I have to read the manual to you."

I sigh. It occurs to me that I've told him about Noah before, about a zillion times, but whatever. There's not much new in our world. Oh, Josh. Everything we've been through and he's still sporting a mullet?

"Oh, come on. We all know the manual by heart."

Josh ignores me and starts his spiel. He sounds like a flight attendant, which, I suppose, he is. "Spinning in a rapidly accelerating capsule causes the blood in your body to flow toward your feet, so remember to tense your muscles to keep some of that blood in your upper regions. Tense your buttocks and legs in order to force the blood back to your head."

"I know that," I say. The trick to getting to the edge of reality is to nearly pass out. I close my eyes in anticipation.

"Time to fly?" Josh asked me. It was my cue.

"Yeppers. Fly me to the stars, Joshie."

I love being strapped down. My heart rate increases as the centrifuge starts to spin. I love the heaviness, the weight. I'm pressed down, spinning into that special place. My mouth will soon be full of dobos torte, the most famous Hungarian cake in the world.

I was the one who discovered that if you loaded your brain with shrooms and hit the centrifuge, you'd taste all your favourite foods as realistically as if you were at a banquet table. I shared my findings with Ani so she too could dine on any pre-nuclear cuisine of her choice. And Ani, being Ani, wanted to share it with everyone. Everyone had to have a turn.

"They'll break the machine," I argued.

"Erzsébet!" I knew she was upset with me when she called me by my Hungarian name instead of "Elizabeth." "We can't keep it for ourselves. It's been a terrible time and they've worked so hard. If I can give them a treat, then I will."

And thus the schedule was drawn up, with everybody having a go if they wanted to, and of course they all did. I wasn't happy to have my visits amputated so the masses could revisit Pizza Hut or Popeyes or McDonald's, but I didn't have a choice.

I was in it only for the dobos. And I'm ready now, ready to bite into the perfect blend of sponge and chocolate and explode with joy.

But nothing happens. Instead, the centrifuge slows down. The skin returns to my face and the weight lifts off my body. What happened? I was on the edge, expecting to fly, only to be left hanging.

"Sorry," Josh mutters and unstraps me. "We've been having some problems lately."

Problems? "Why didn't you tell me?"

"Because I made some adjustments and hoped it would be okay. I know how important this is to you. Do you want to try again?"

"Are you sure it won't spin off and kill me?"

"It can't kill you. It just might not work."

I lie down and close my eyes. The dobos. I need to go there, particularly if it's the very last time. If I have to live out the rest of my life eating seaweed, jellyfish, and eels, with a side of hardy cabbage and a few pseudo-cereals thrown in for good measure, I need one last sugar rush and I'm going to make sure it's a good one.

"Hand me my purse," I say. I confer with the clown, only this time I chew on a couple of bennies and all my synapses are instantly on high alert.

"I'm ready," I say to Josh. "Come on, sunshine, we don't want to miss the window. Timing is everything."

He rushes over and straps me in. I'm feeling awesome. Cotton-woolly and soft, ready to fly.

The machine starts to spin. I beg it silently, *Come on, baby — one last time. Take me back to the dobos.* I try to see it, in my mind's eye.

Instead, I see Nagypapa.

I'm spinning faster and faster but still, there is no dobos. Only my grandparents and their house, that fragrant house, redolent of lamb's wool, freshly ground coffee, sliced salami, and dark chocolate.

Now I'm standing in their living room. My grandparents are hosting a party. It's 1979 and I'm thirteen. I'm wearing a blue dress with tiny black flowers and I feel so powerful. My whole life lies ahead of me and I'm going to ride it with style.

My father arrives. He guides the famous guest into the room and a hush falls. The guest is some guy named Edward Teller, a famous scientist. Ostracized by other scientists, my father had told me, but welcomed by my grandfather. I hope Edward, the famous guest, will like the dobos that Nagymama and I made together.

Edward Teller, the inventor of the hydrogen bomb.

I'm spinning and spinning in the centrifuge. I'm pressed down and I want to get off it but I can't stop it and I can't move. Why haven't I remembered that I'd met Edward Teller? Why didn't Ani remind me?

The centrifuge spins and I'm back in the living room and my father is across the room. I go to him, pull him by the arm, and lead him into the kitchen, which smells of rye bread, sliced meat, and red wine.

"Why is he here?" I hiss at my father.

My father shrugs. "I told you he was coming. Your head is always in the clouds — you didn't listen. Teller's an ardent anti-Communist, a Soviet-hater, and a fellow Hungarian who went to school in Hungary at the same time as Nagypapa. They have a common background."

"He invented the hydrogen bomb!"

"If he hadn't, someone else would have. Come on, come back to the party. Teller's an interesting man — you should talk to him."

We go back to the living room and I watch Teller. He is laughing and joking.

Nagymama asks me to hand out pieces of the cake and when I get to Teller, I hand him a plate with a large slice and I watch him take a bite.

It's just him and me. The rest of the room falls away. I am spinning and pressed down and there's Teller, standing in front of me, eating cake and smiling.

"Very good dobos torte," he says. He shovels the cake in, chewing and talking, waving his fork in the air.

I see his mouth moving, his mouth that is full of cake, but I can't hear what he's saying. It's like I'm underwater, at the bottom of a swimming pool. The world is muted and moving in slow motion.

Teller hands me his plate and hurries across the room and the party chatter starts up again as if a door has opened and a crowd rushed in.

Nagymama appears and takes the empty plate and hands me a large slice of cake.

"It's the last one," she says.

I look down at it. It is the last one, but I can't eat it. I'd rather have seaweed and jellyfish and eels. Try to grow strawberries in the hydroponic garden. Anything but dobos.

The centrifuge shudders to a stop and I lie there.

"Was it okay?" Josh asks, peering at me, his face close to mine.

"It was weird. Not like before."

"I'm sorry," Josh says as he unties the straps. "I should have looped you in that it was failing. I just hoped it would be okay."

I take his hand and climb off the table. "It doesn't matter," I tell him. "I think I'm ready to move on."

I turn and look at the machine as I leave. "Lock the door and don't let anyone in," I say to Josh. "It had a good run. I believe it's time to watch a magnificent sunset and partake of the new batch of white lightning the brewery's been cooking up."

"A party!" Josh is delighted and I'm glad I've made him happy.

"It is my birthday," I remind him.

"We haven't forgotten," he says.

Later, when we are gathered to watch the sunset, the cook surprises me with a small, lopsided cake, topped with lit beeswax candles. The rest of the crew sing "Happy Birthday" with gusto.

"It's unusual," the cook apologizes for the cake. "But I did my best."

"I'm sure it will be wonderful," I assure her.

We cut careful slices and the others watch as I take a bite.

"It's not a dobos," the cook apologizes again, and I shake my head.

"You're right, it's not."

The cook's face falls.

"It's so much better." And I really mean it. It's fresh and tangy and new.

The cook's face lights up.

"How grateful am I," I say to the others, "to be alive. We don't know how long we've got left but we'll fight to the very end. And we'll do it together."

I'm seventy-fucking-five and I'm still here. And I'm good with that.

A VIEW WORTH ALL THE AQUA IN THE WORLD

Anuja Varghese

You have found something special. Something very old. You found it in the underground, which is full of old things, but this is not a kind of thing you've seen before. It is some kind of oldtech artifact. It does not connect to any networks, as far as you can tell. It appears to be several soft screens in a hard outer case. There are lines and lines of old code on each screen, but they are frozen in place. You jabbed at the symbols with the pads of your sensors. You looked for a reset button. You tried to swipe past the first fixed screen, but that tore it apart. You consider, for a moment, opening the hatch of your Personal Protective Pod so you can handle the artifact with your hands. Whatever material these old screens are made of is very delicate. You pull up a toxicity scan on the PPP dashboard, but the numbers fluctuate wildly as you turn in a slow circle. You bought this pod used and it was an outdated model even then. The data is unreliable. You keep the hatch closed.

Instead, you deposit the artifact carefully into the PPP's outer containment compartment. If you could activate the thing, you might be able to run the code. Most oldtech is useless, although you seem to have a knack for finding bits and pieces that are worth just enough Aqua to get by. You have heard that Off-World some people will pay good Aqua for old-world relics. You don't know what they're building out there, but you have a feeling that this time you have found something that will help — something they will want. You imagine entering your unit and there, lined up against the wall, you can see them: 5-Gallon Aqua jugs, bright blue and beautiful. Enough to last you a month, maybe more. Enough leftover for a meal from a Virtual Nutrition Station. You can picture how Gator's face will light up when you tell him. It's been a long time since you were able to eat any real food together.

You follow the tracks in the underground until stone walls turn to white tile and you see the faded red crest of the overlapping white trees and crescent moon. A few months ago, everyone in your building contributed a bit of Aqua and now there is a holographic tree outside the main entrance. It has white flowers, faintly tinged with pink. It gives off a sweet, synthetic fragrance. The symbols at the base of its trunk spell out "CHERRY BLOSSOM TREE" (genus *Prunus*, also known as Sakura tree, extinct 2425). You didn't have the Aqua to contribute to the purchase, but you like to think you're helping with the tree's upkeep by stopping to reboot it whenever the whole thing starts to flicker. Gator says a kid in his EduPod told him there used to be rows and rows of *real* trees just like this one, right here in Toronto. You didn't disagree because he seemed so enchanted by the idea, but you're pretty sure it's a myth, like "lakes" or "animals." Most of the surviving information about pre-WW12 civilizations has been taken Off-World, so there's no way to know for sure. But as you pass the crest on the wall and climb the stairs into the daylight, you have a momentary vision of a wild, ancient city full of trees growing right from the ground; great expanses of free, fresh Aqua; and small, winged creatures sailing overhead. It takes you a minute, but you conjure the word for the fairy-tale beasts you're picturing: *Birds.* Almost everyone is named after some type of "animal" now; such is the human fascination with those maybe-mythic creatures that maybe once walked the earth. You are no exception and you did no different when you had the choice, but still — you cannot help but think there is a danger in naming humans after creatures that, by slaughter or starvation or acts of vengeful gods, eventually all went extinct.

You cross the street and touch your sensors to one of the security screens embedded in the stone pillars on either side of the iron gate. The screen flashes red, the symbols showing "INSUFFICIENT AQUA." You sigh and pull up your contacts on the PPP dashboard. You touch Bear's face on the screen and in a few seconds, his picture is replaced by his actual face. He looks tired, and also as if seeing you is not helping.

"What do you want, Bee?" he asks.

"I'm at the gate," you say. "Let me in. I found something."

He shakes his head. "More *treasure* from the underground? Whatever oldtech shit you've dragged up here is probably worthless — you know that. You keep coming here with Gallons in your eyes, and then I gotta be the bad guy and send you away with Millilitres in your hands. It's not worth it, Bee."

"Don't you want to see what it is?" You try not to smile, saying this. You already know Bear's curiosity will get the better of him.

Bear hesitates, then relents, muttering under his breath. His face disappears and a moment later, the security screen flashes green and the gates swing open.

"Welcome to High Park Trade Zone, sponsored by NorthCorps!" a friendly, feminine voice from the screen ushers you inside. "You are Guest four hundred and forty-nine. You have sixty minutes to complete your business in High Park Trade Zone, sponsored by NorthCorps. Have a great day!"

The NorthCorps logo appears on your PPP dashboard, along with a sixty-minute countdown.

You move quickly, past the rows of concrete buildings rising from bone-dry, cracked earth; past the holographic trees; past the Automatic Aqua Machines; past the endless NorthCorps ads. NorthCorps used to sell clothes. Then it started to sell tech. Then it bought all the VN Stations, and now that VN is how everybody eats (or wants to), NorthCorps is something between corporation and government, the multicoloured stripes of its logo as prominent above ground as the red and white trees and crescent moon underground.

You find Bear's building, but before you can lift your sensors to the security pad on the door, it swings open and a mother and two children spill outside. You cannot help but stare. Their PPPs shimmer around them, barely visible, as if they are just walking in the open air. You cannot even imagine the amount of Aqua something like that must cost. The children chase each other, screeching and laughing. Their hair shines and their lips aren't cracked. They are so *hydrated*. The mother catches your eye and smiles. Her teeth are still white. The children were, of course, the first clue, but the teeth make it clear that she has eaten VN all her life. There are all kinds of AquaSub now, but no matter the brand or flavour of the thick, gritty, synthetic syrup that has become the world's source of food, one thing remains the same: if you drink it straight, along with the infertility, dry mouth, rashes, and hair loss, it will also rot your teeth. The VN-AquaSub, on the other hand, is colourless, odourless, tasteless; an entirely different and far pricier synthetic compound. It's not a big deal either way, purely aesthetic these days — between AquaSub and VN, nobody has that much need for teeth anymore, anyway. But Gator's teeth are still white, still strong. And you're going to do everything you can to keep them that way. If you can get this one thing right for him, well, that's something at least.

You return the mother's smile with a nod, hiding your own blackened, gap-toothed gums, and hurry inside. Bear's shop is toward the back of the building. He is a long-time tenant in High Park. Most days, you would call him a friend. You hope today is one of those days.

Bear sells Virtual Reality Vacations. His shop is made up of six VR chairs, each behind a black curtain to give the potential customer some privacy in which to connect their PPP to the chair and sample any number of vacation destinations. There are group packages, family packages, honeymoon packages. Some even come with VN add-ons.

A holographic couple seated at a table appears in front of you. The man reaches across the table, kisses the back of the woman's hand. They clink full glasses of sparkling Aqua, then crack open the glistening red claws on their plates. The woman closes her eyes and licks moist lips. "Mmmmmm," she says.

The hologram emits a scent that your sensors pick up, scan for toxins, and transmit into your PPP. It is rich and briny and buttery all at once. You have never smelled anything like it, but it is making your mouth water with wanting.

The holographic man looks in your direction and smiles, as if for the first time noticing you are there. He leans toward you with an eyebrow raised. "What are you waiting for?" he asks. "Book your Cape Cod VR getaway today."

You see Bear through the hologram as it begins to flicker out. "What is it?" you ask.

Bear briefly looks up from the gaming band embedded in his wrist. "Lobster," he says.

Lobster. You'll remember that.

You approach the counter and he feigns disinterest, one eye on his game, one eye on you. "So. Whadd'ya got?"

You pull the artifact from the containment compartment and put it on the counter. You open its cover. You flip from screen to screen as gently as you can, but even still, one of them disintegrates a bit beneath your sensors. You have Bear's full attention now.

"Stop touching it," he says.

He pushes a button under the counter and a sliding screen slowly moves across the entrance to the shop. You hear the "store closed" loop beginning on the outward-facing side of the screen; a cheerful VR Vacation sales rep (definitely not Bear) apologizes for the inconvenience and offers customers a virtual tour of current bestselling, low-Aqua VR Vacation options. You've heard it before. You have, after all, been an after-hours guest in High Park many times. But you and Bear, you're not doing that anymore. You said, *It's too hard for Gator.* You thought, *It's too hard for me.*

The screen seals off the shop from the rest of the building. Another push of a button, and a detoxifying chemical mist jets out of the ceiling. Bear calls up a tox scan on his PPP dashboard and you do the same.

"All good?" he asks.

"All good," you say, and swipe your dashboard closed before he notices that the numbers your PPP is showing make no sense. The fine for Personal Protective Pod Malfunction is 500 Gallons, which is beyond the realm of possibility for you. But, depending on what this thing you have found is, you might finally have enough to fix your PPP, have Aqua to spare, *and* take Gator to a VN Station. Your proximity to that kind of relief, to giving Gator the pleasure of real food, is nearly unbearable.

You and Bear open the hatches of your pods at the same time; his slides open smoothly, you crank yours open with a handle that's fallen off twice. The flexiglass barrier folds down in sections, finally snapping into a neat cube at your feet. You look Bear over. You allow yourself this. Black hair, black skin, black teeth, black eyes — he is a beautiful man. There is an intimacy to seeing each other like this again, outside of PPPs, and it is familiar and awkward and with no dashboard to fumble with, you don't know where to look or what to do with your hands.

"It's good to see you, Bee," Bear says.

"Good to see you too," you say. *Can't go down this road again.* You clear your throat. "So, what do you think it is?"

Bear handles the artifact delicately, his fingers skimming lightly over the lines of illegible code. Ah, too close, that. Too close to fingers skimming skin. You look away.

He holds up his wrist and the gaming band scans the artifact. "Still got Gator in that NorthCorps EduPod?" he asks. His tone is nonchalant; the question is not.

You shrug. "It's free."

"Is it? By the time their system spits that boy out, he'll be fully brandwashed, ready and willing to be a loyal NorthCorps slave — sorry, *customer* — for life."

"If it's his impressionable mind they want, instead of Aqua I don't have, well —"

"Some things are worth more than Aqua, Bee."

You could laugh. Or else slap his stubbled cheek. Does he know how many times you have had to choose between keeping the connectivity on in your unit and having enough AquaSub for you and Gator both? Does he know you have been dehydrated for months? Does he see the patches where your hair is falling out and your skin is flaking off? He does not, and his blindness makes you cruel. "Thank you for your concern, but you're not his father," you say.

He could say, *And you're not his mother. You're just some lonely woman who found a little boy abandoned in the underground and instead of turning him in to the authorities, you kept him, called him your own.* He could say that. But he says nothing.

The band fused to the bones of his wrist lights up. He checks its screen, looks at the artifact, looks back at the screen. He gives a low whistle.

"I'll be damned," he says. "It's a book."

You don't know what that means, but it's making your heart beat faster. "How do you activate it?" you ask.

Bear laughs. "You don't. It's oldtech but, like, *really* old. Whatever this stuff is" — he caresses the first screen — "it sure as hell can't hold up to Toronto air." He closes the shell. "It's probably this hard cover that preserved so much of the code in the underground for so long. I've never seen so much of it and all still in sequence, I think."

"Can you run the code?"

"Me? No way. Something like this ..."

You wait, holding your breath.

"… Something like this, I call my Off-World guy."

You are shaking a little; the relief flooding your body is an overwhelming warmth. The Off-World Aqua that will fill up your unit in big, blue, overflowing jugs is so vivid in your mind and on your tongue that you can almost feel it. It is clear and quenching. If you had the tears to spare, you might cry.

"Call him," you say.

Bear is watching the screen at his wrist. When he looks up at you, his expression is a bit stunned. "I already did."

He turns his wrist to face you, and you see the number of Gallons his Off-World contact is offering for this oldtech thing, this *book*. It is so much more than you dared to hope. When you have imagined this moment of extraordinary, miraculous luck before, you always pictured yourself cool, casually gracious. *Sure, make the deal. Tell your guy to take a Litre off the top for his trouble.* The reality of more Aqua than you know what to do with leaves you breathless and speechless and clutching the edge of Bear's counter because your legs feel holographic, like they might flicker out from underneath you at any moment.

Bear comes around the counter and puts his arms around you. "Breathe, Bee," he says.

You lean into him and let him hold you up. All you can hear is his heartbeat. All you can feel is your own thirst.

———

You take Gator to the VN Station at the base of the NorthCorps Tower. You have lived in Toronto all your life but have never had the Aqua to take the elevator to the top. It has been bombed and built back up countless times over the past centuries, and now it remains standing, a historic monument to ancient Toronto. There isn't much to it, you think. But then, seeing Gator's glee as he takes in the whole city from above, it is worth every drop of the Half-Gallon the two tickets cost.

You touch his shoulder and whether it's the sensitivity of your new sensors or the barely there flexiglass of his newtech PPP, it feels almost as if you have touched his bare shoulder with your bare hand. Gator, predictably, was over the novelty of the newtech in a day, but you are still awestruck by all of it. You move hesitantly in your new PPP, as if any swipe of the dashboard might cause the whole thing to disintegrate, like the screens in the book that you found, which is now in a capsule to its Off-World home. *Not screens*, Bear told you later. *Pages.*

"Ready, Gator?" you ask.

He turns at your touch and grins. The same alert that has popped up on your dashboard has popped up on his as well. *Your reserved ports at the NorthCorps Tower VN Station are now ready. Please proceed to the Station.*

He rolls his eyes in typical nine-year-old fashion. "Mom, we've been over this," he tells you, patiently, like he is the one talking to a child, not you. "Gator is a baby name. Everyone calls me Alli now, okay?"

You pretend to think. Then, "No can do, kiddo," you say. "You'll always be Gator to me."

He groans but it is good-natured. "Let's go," he says, "before they give our ports away."

He leads the way, so confident, as if he has been here hundreds of times before. He has the golden-brown skin and coarse, black curls to suggest he came from people who look like you or like Bear or like the two of you combined. It's not the reason you kept him. But it's not *not* the reason, either.

At the VN Station, you touch your sensors to the Reservations screen and it lights up green, your port numbers flashing. You have taken Gator to smaller stations before. You have shared VN hamburgers and ice cream — a whole cheese pizza between you once. But the tech keeps getting better and the price keeps going up and you can hardly remember the last time you ate real food, instead of guzzling sickly-sweet AquaSub straight from the tube.

Gator is trying to play it cool as he settles into the plush VN chair and connects his PPP to the port in the side of the chair, but you can see how he glows with excitement. His happiness settles over you like a salve, already healing the parts of you that have been rubbed raw by scarcity.

A bored-looking teenager approaches your chairs, holding two sets of silver canisters with symbols denoting "VN-AQUASUB-NORTHCORPS STATION 008." As she drops the canisters into their slots in the arms of your chairs, she recites, "Welcome to the NorthCorps Tower VN Station, Toronto's best VN Dining Experience. My name's Fawn — I'll be your UX moderator today. Can I start you with some fresh Aqua?"

Gator glances at you and you nod. Then he nods too. You can see how easily he will wear the sheen of wealth, how it becomes him.

"Off-World or ocean?" Fawn asks.

"Off-World," you say. *Why not?*

Your old PPP had an attachment that came in through the containment compartment where you could connect a feeding tube and wrestle it to your mouth. The new PPP has its own sleek feeding tube that extends silently from the dashboard, lining up perfectly with your lips. You tuck it into the inside of your cheek and lean back in the chair. You wait.

The chair vibrates faintly beneath you, its sensors syncing with yours. The inner walls of your PPP go black and then clear, and you and Gator are in the VN simulation together. You are back at the top of the Tower. You sit across from each other, a pitcher of Aqua between you. You pour some into his glass and some into your glass and you both drink. The real, Off-World Aqua that Fawn has fed into your ports filters through the feeding tube and into your mouth, almost, but not quite exactly, synced with your motion of drinking. It is so good. So cold. No trace of salt. No hint of cloying sweetness. You have an account at a tank now — you can pull Aqua from any Automatic Aqua Machine anywhere, anytime. And yet, you cannot imagine ever getting used to luxury like this.

You touch the menu screen on your side of the table, and Gator does the same on his. He orders a basket of bread, which appears on the table between you in seconds. You pick up one of the rolls, and even though you know your hand is empty, it looks real and smells real and when you take a bite, the VN-AquaSub that floods your mouth is warm and soft and tastes as real as anything you have ever known. *Bread.*

Gator orders a hamburger and fries (a safe choice) and tries pasta with tomato sauce (a foray into the unknown), and a triple-layer, triangular slab of chocolate cake.

You joke, *Looks like you've got more icing than cake there, pal.*

He makes a show of being shocked, hands pressed to his cheeks. *How did they know? That's just how I like it!*

You laugh and you eat and you can hear the machinery of the chair working as the canisters of VN-AquaSub empty into your feeding tube, a quiet hum that is easy to ignore. You have ordered the lobster, now that you know what it is, and it is every bit as satisfying as the Cape Cod couple suggested it would be.

Gator is already thinking of the next meal, asking which VN Station you want to go to next. You want to try everything: Butter chicken and apple pie. A faucet for your unit that pours Aqua on demand. Dim sum. New teeth. Filet mignon. All the food you have heard of and all the food you haven't. The possibilities are endless.

The simulation runs a sunset as it nears its end, casting Gator's curls in an orange glow. You savour your last bites of lobster, and he finishes off his cake. Your canisters are empty, your feeding tubes retract. You are both so full, so nourished. The VN simulation is fading, its last image a darkened sky outside the NorthCorps Tower, Gator's bright smile, and the city glittering all around you as far as the eye can see.

YOU NEED A LICENCE FOR THAT

Sifton Tracey Anipare

For Ewurasi, who would have been a great mom.

Emma jostled the vegetable platter in her gloved hands and elbowed the doorbell for the third time. Inside the house she heard several women laugh, as if they were mocking her on cue. She watched another sigh mist in front of her face, struggle for corporeal form in the chilly night air, and inevitably fail. Maybe it wasn't too late to head back down the street and catch the next LRT — after all, it came every 5.08 minutes — but then the curtains in the front window jostled and wrenched apart. Several faces leered around the corner, noticed Emma on the porch, then exchanged wary glances.

"Yes, geniuses, *get the door*, please," Emma muttered to herself. Her stomach trembled against the silicone container. She could have sworn she heard the carrot sticks bounce around. "I know, I know," she blurted out loud. It probably would have been better to just abandon the platter on the porch and let the Crosstown mutants — a.k.a. "squigeons" — have at it. But she'd come all this way. It'd be pointless to go back hungry for nothing.

Still, the dark stretch of road, lined with expensive hydrocars, looked very enticing.

The sound of locks whirring and an unfamiliar high-pitched giggle on the other side of the door jolted Emma back to attention. She swept away thoughts of fleeing, straightened up, and forced herself to smile. The door cracked open, no more than an inch.

A suspicious pair of eyes peered out. "Can I help you?"

"Um … sorry, is this not Adrianna's place?"

The eyes widened with relief as the door opened fully. "Emma!" A woman about her age, in a sheer cocktail dress, embraced her. "Holy shit, I barely recognized you!"

"Oh. That's okay. I guess."

"Come in, come in! I'm so glad you could make it — wait. It's just you?" Adrianna pretended to pout. "You didn't bring anyone? Your husband, boyfriend?"

Emma reinforced her smile. "It's just me."

"Aw, that's too bad! Oh, well. Here, let me help you with that." Adrianna slammed the door with one hand while the other began to unzip Emma's heavy coat without hesitation.

Emma tried to maintain her polite smile as she manoeuvred the platter from one hand to the other. Adrianna had always been extra, back in the day. Apparently not much had changed.

"'Bout time you showed up. I was starting to think you'd bailed, just like — whoa, what on *earth* is that?" Adrianna gaped at Emma's turtleneck sweater dress. "Are you *actually* wearing cotton?"

Emma made a face. What was wrong with her? "It's just hemp."

"*Oh.*" Adrianna made a strange gesture with her hand. "I was about to say ... never mind. You look *amazing*!"

"Thanks. You look ..."

Adrianna smirked. She pretended to clear her throat as she stroked her neckline, where Emma could see a series of thick black lines peeking up from the collar of her dress.

"... amazing, as always," Emma finished.

"Why, thank you! Now, come — this way!"

Adrianna clamped her fingers down on Emma's shoulders and herded her through the crowd. Emma had not been expecting so many guests — certainly not so many women in various stages of pregnancy. She found herself being pushed through a large group of people, at least four of whom had significant baby bumps. They were all studying a woman with a large patch of white gauze taped to her chest. Despite the redness brimming around the patch, everyone was taking turns poking at it. Adrianna whispered something to her as they passed, and she burst into giggles. Like birds of prey, the other women's heads turned to watch the hostess and the new arrival move along.

"There's *plenty*, as I'm sure you've already guessed." Adrianna tugged at Emma's platter. "What are those — veggies? Aw, those would have made a great appetizer! But it's fine, I'm sure someone will enjoy them."

"Oh. Sorry. I didn't realize —" Emma thought hard. "I could have sworn you told me seven."

"Did I?" Adrianna waved her hand again. "My bad. Preemptive case of 'mom brain,' ha ha! Most everyone here has to get their little ones to bed early. You know how it is. Oh, wait, no, I guess you don't, but you know what I mean! Here, let's move this stuff over. Geez, Emma, look at all these — your garden must be *humongous!*"

Emma was only half listening, glancing around the room while Adrianna moved plates around on the long, elegant table. Clearly the party had been going for a while, but there was still plenty of food left. The way Adrianna was talking, Emma surmised she must have doubled the number of estimated guests since their last exchange. There were far more than "a dozen or so" between the living room and kitchen, and Emma heard children running and screaming from the floor above.

She tuned back into Adrianna's voice when she heard her name. "Huh? Oh, my garden. Well, actually —"

"There. That looks perfect!" Adrianna clapped for herself. "They'll go great with the protein cups, which you have *got* to try! Just a couple, of course — can't have you maxing out your Breathalyzer, right?" She reached to grab a large biodegradable plate, then shook her head and grabbed one of the smaller ones. "Sorry — 'mom brain,' again!" Adrianna sang.

Emma looked around at the guests, more thoroughly this time. "Where's Grace?" she asked.

"Oh, she bailed, like a while ago. Got rushed to 'emerg,' but turns out it was just her first Braxton Hicks. Anyway, they took ages to discharge her, so she's chilling at home. What a loser."

A woman and a man holding a fussy baby ran up to Adrianna just then, their coats already on as they explained they had to go. The baby screamed and snatched her father's phone right off his face.

"Yup, definitely someone's bedtime!" The woman laughed.

"Shit." The man picked up the dark smartphone glasses off the floor. "Okay, good. Thought she cancelled the Uber. It's already outside."

"Bye, Anna. Lovely party!" The woman kissed Adrianna's cheeks, then Adrianna walked the couple to the door, leaving Emma to fend for herself.

Emma didn't mind. The spread was lovely. She hadn't seen this much food in one place in decades. She helped herself to some carrots, broccoli, and cauliflower, then carried her plate around to the other side of the table, careful not to look at her vegetables again. Maybe if she put some distance between them, no one else would ask where they came from. Plus, it gave her an excuse to check out the super-fancy protein cups, the lab-grown pigs in a blanket, and the array of mushroom sausage and lentil pepperoni on a charcuterie board that took up most of the table. Her stomach growled as she passed each dish, as if it would reach out and grab them if it could. But Adrianna had given Emma a small plate. The last thing Emma wanted was to draw attention to herself. She was getting enough curious looks already, being the only visibly single woman there.

For a party with so many licensed women, there were a lot of cheese options — cheese cubes, cheese slices, cheese logs, even cheese balls, and three different kinds of fondue. Each dish had a little sign in front of it: Oat Milk, Potato Milk, Certified Pasteurized, London Fog, St. Micheline. There was a long plate of sliders labelled, "YES, we printed these ourselves!," next to a giant basket marked "Truffle-Oil Fries (RIP truffles!)."

And then there were the desserts. Nothing looked local. There were dozens of different-coloured macarons, a platter heaped with meringues, several stands jammed with retro-style cake pops, and even the remaining lower half of a cro-quembouche. But what caught Emma's eye was a long, sturdy, rectangular yellow sponge that sat in the middle of it all. It took Emma a moment to realize it might be a cake. She felt the inside of her mouth get soft. She was salivating. As politely as she could, she located a spatula (probably intended for the CBD cauliflower pizza beside it) and picked it up.

Something large and heavy rammed into Emma's back. "Whoa!"

Emma turned to see a man in dark smartphone glasses behind her. The man let out an angry sigh as he gave up on pushing her and went around Emma to grab a handful of carrots and drop them onto a small plate. "There. *Satisfied?*"

Emma was about to respond when a small boy ran up to the man and snatched the plate away. The man followed, saying more but never once looking back at Emma. It was as if she didn't exist. She turned back to the table and saw three women helping themselves to the yellow sponge, making slow, steady cuts and finishing their elaborate sentences before they put their servings on plates. Emma shook her head, trying not to look frazzled. She'd come back later.

Emma took a few more meringues and a couple of in vitro scallops swathed in lemon garlic butter. She tried her best not to look too eager and excited, but she must have given herself away because every time she excused herself to the women standing around the table, they gave her strange looks. She smiled and nodded back in greeting, only to receive quick glances down at her turtleneck, raised eyebrows, and turned backs.

Maybe I'll just stay a couple of hours, Emma thought. *No big deal.*

"Oh, my gosh, Emma, I completely forgot to give you this!" Adrianna appeared at her shoulder with a tall flute of sparkling pink gold. "I'm such a shitty hostess — I didn't even get you a drink. Here. You've *got* to try it — it's called Prosecco rosé. It's this sparkling wine from Italy —"

"Oh, thanks. I know it. I'm actually good —"

"*No*, you're not. Here!" Adrianna smacked the scallop tongs out of Emma's grip, lifted her hand, and pushed the stem of the glass into it. "It's *so* good — you've *never* had anything better in your life. Trust me! Now, go mingle!"

Adrianna turned Emma around and pushed her away from the table, immediately distracted by her husband asking her about finding extra somethings or other before Emma could comment on having no one to mingle with. Everyone was in their own little cluster and didn't look open to someone squeezing into their conversations.

Emma took a few steps around the living room, looking for a place where she could sit and balance her food, but saw nothing. She considered claiming a corner, but they all appeared to be occupied by tall, dour-looking men submerged in their screentime. Emma stopped in front of the fireplace and put her glass of Prosecco on the ledge to free one of her hands, but when she reached for a carrot stick, three screaming kids ran by, almost knocking into her. She dodged their flailing fists in the nick of time.

"Elsa! Ariel!" A woman stormed after them, and Emma managed to dodge her flailing hands just in time too. "What did I say! *Walking feet!*"

Forty-five minutes, Emma thought. *Surely I can handle that much.*

Two of the children turned back to the woman, then took each other's hands and demonstrated "walking feet" as they joined whatever chaos was happening upstairs.

The woman returned to Emma's side. "Sorry. You'd think they'd know better, but let them stay out after dark and look what happens."

"No worries. I'm used to it."

"Oh?"

"Yeah, I used to work at a community centre. Runners. Got them all the time."

The woman smiled. "Say, are you Emma?"

Emma smiled back. "I am."

The woman extended her elbow in lieu of a handshake. "So lovely to meet you! I'm Maya. Adrianna told us about you."

"'Us'?"

"Yeah, she has quite the gathering here tonight. Lots of girlfriends with tons of questions about the whole licensing thing. I mean, obviously there's a bunch of us who've got ours, but when it comes to the test …" Maya shrugged, surveying the room.

Emma couldn't help glancing down at Maya's neckline. Three black stripes peeked above her collar.

"So, Adrianna mentioned inviting a government employee tonight. You know, someone who might have a few tips!"

"Oh … well, I don't know how much help I'll be."

"That's okay. Think of it as an excuse to stay closer to the food." She winked as she led Emma away from the fireplace. Then she stopped and pointed. "Wait, is that your drink back there?"

Emma shook her head. "Nope."

"Just making sure."

Emma followed Maya to the centre of the room, where a group of women chatted around a coffee table. Except for two women on the couch, all wore 3-D–printed tops and dresses that exposed at least some of the black bars on their chests. One of them had to have the same tattoo, because she was at least eight months along. "Rachelle, relax," she was saying to the other woman, patting her knee. "You *know* you'd make a great mom!"

The other woman flinched. "I don't *need* a fucking licence to tell me that, Chloe!"

Maya must have seen it too. She slowed her pace and approached the group with her arm open toward Emma, to indicate that everyone needed to shut up and be civil for a moment. "Friends, this is Emma."

Pretending she hadn't noticed anything, Emma shook elbows with the women standing next to Maya, who introduced themselves as Olivia, Sophia, and Chloe. (Rachelle, who was pointedly taking an extensive sip of her drink, did not introduce herself.)

The pregnant woman — Chloe — seemed to perk up a little. "Like, *the* Emma?"

Emma smiled, nervous. What exactly had Adrianna told them to make her so famous? "Yes?"

"Adrianna's told us *so* much about you! Um ..." Sophia narrowed her eyes at Emma's turtleneck dress. "She didn't mention you were into vintage, though."

Everyone turned to stare at Emma, now. A few nearby guests even tugged at their collars and sleeves as if they were causing them discomfort.

"It's hemp," Emma just said.

"*Oh!*" They laughed, relieved.

Chloe studied Emma with a friendly, curious look. "Adrianna said you worked for the government for, what was it, ten, fifteen years?"

Everyone seemed to perk up at this news.

"No." Emma laughed. "Why would she say that? I mean, I used to work at a community centre library, but that's not —"

"They still *have* those?" Rachelle's tone was neither friendly nor curious.

Maya's glance shifted between her and Emma. "Yes," she said in a patient voice. "There's still quite a few in the city. There's one just down the street from me. Elsa and Ariel go there with their dad all the time."

"Hmm." Olivia tapped her fork against her lips in thought. "I wonder why Adrianna said you did something with the government. Oh, well. That's too bad."

Why? Emma wondered.

"So, what do you do now?" asked Chloe, interrupting Emma's thoughts.

"I'm an archivist at Thomas Fisher."

"Oh. That's ... interesting." Rachelle blinked several times. "*Very* vintage. And your husband?"

It was Emma's turn to blink. "I'm not married."

"*Oh.*"

Everyone looked down at their feet, or their empty plates. Even with all the loud conversations and sounds of children at play upstairs, the awkward silence was deafening to Emma. Her eyes darted to the kitchen. It looked less populated. Maybe now was a good time to sneak some of that spongy thing onto her plate. Then she looked down. She hadn't touched any of her food. There was no way she'd get away with it.

She decided to change the subject — something that could get them all talking to each other long enough to let her stuff her face. "So, what do you all do?" she asked, before putting a buttery scallop into her mouth.

"Oh, nothing exciting," Maya joked. "Rachelle's in information management. Olivia and Sophia are systems analysts, and Chloe and I are stay-at-homes." She paused. "For the record, I think it's nice we still have libraries. I remember when

One World said everyone should bring them back. Thought they'd go the way of the killer bee, you know?"

"Huh?" said Chloe.

"You know, extinct?"

Sophia made a face. "But can you call it 'extinct' if they disappeared and then came back?"

"I guess not." Maya shrugged. "But bees are different. They technically didn't go *extinct* extinct. There was that whole Sask-African invasion in the States, remember?"

"Oh, yeah." Chloe rolled her eyes. "Sorry — 'mom brain'!"

All the women giggled, except Emma (and Rachelle, who did not look very entertained, either). "Mom brain" seemed to be their inside joke.

Closer to the kitchen, a glass fell and shattered. "I meant to put that there!" said a deep voice. Again, everyone laughed. Someone's husband, Emma presumed.

"Too bad Emma's not a teacher," Emma heard Chloe murmur in Rachelle's ear. "I hear teachers can pass like *that*!"

"No, no — not anymore. You're thinking back too far. Maybe in the first trial years, the tests were super easy. But now?" Rachelle snorted. "I might as well be applying to work for NASA."

Emma finished her last protein cup and turned toward Maya, who was now talking about the latest scandal, and began working on her sausage and pepperoni. She nodded in all the right places as she ate and feigned surprise that another influencer couple's pre-licence *mukbang* had been found on the Dark Web. Emma had never paid much attention to celebrity news, but she was now genuinely curious about what the pair had eaten to earn the most severe sentence in licensing history.

Rachelle's loud sigh distracted her. "Wish I could try some of the rosé. That's the second glass George's poured for himself."

Chloe said, "Why don't you? Your test isn't until Monday."

"I know. I just want to play it safe. In case I actually pass this time. Third time's a charm, right?" Rachelle was sarcastic.

"But it's not like you're going to get *pregnant* by Monday —"

"I *know*, but still!" Rachelle let out a huff. "I wish I was still single. Must be nice."

"Well, not if you have to breathalyze."

"Oh, yeah. You're right. That's less fun."

Chloe was about to laugh but then noticed Emma was listening. She cleared her throat instead. Rachelle shifted in her seat. Emma's stomach hurt.

Maya noticed Emma's discomfort and put a friendly hand on her shoulder. "I heard you brought that amazing veggie platter."

That got everyone's attention.

"Wow, that was you?" Olivia asked. "Your rooftop must be huge, to grow so much! Where exactly do you live?"

"Yeah, our condo would never let one person harvest that much!" Sophia said. "Are you in the suburbs or something?"

"Wait," Rachelle cut in. "You're not married. How did you even manage all that work by yourself?"

Emma got flustered. "Oh. Well. No. I mean, I live downtown. But my building is too old for a rooftop garden, so —"

"Wait. Did you get them from ... a *store*?"

Everyone froze in horror. Chloe looked at the broccoli she'd just picked up from her plate as if it was a live grenade covered in kerosene. Rachelle looked like she was about to snatch it from the pregnant woman and punch Emma in the face with it.

"They're Ontario certified," she explained. "The broccoli is from Ingersoll?"

The women sighed, and even giggled like it had all been a delightful joke.

"Phew!" Chloe rubbed her swollen stomach. "I mean, I *know* almost everything is local now, but you know ... Carpenter and I can't take any risks!"

"So, you're not even going to try the desserts?" Sophia pretended to gasp. "You're kidding. Adrianna lined up for *hours* to get them!"

Olivia shook her head. "Honey, at least try the castella. She can't get another permit until next year!"

"What's the 'castella'?" Emma asked.

"It's that giant spongy thing there." Maya pointed. "Adrianna found it in the Asian department at FCBO. It's imported and expensive as hell, yeah, but it's One World certified. Reminds you of those old-school yellow dish sponges, doesn't it? Don't let that fool you. You should try it!" She eyed Emma's full plate but continued to smile. "Just be sure your Breathalyzer can take it."

"Oh." Emma did her best to smile back. "It's okay. I didn't eat much today. Because I knew I was coming here. I mean —"

"Oh, good! That's smart." Maya gave her a conspiratorial nod toward the table. "You should be fine, then."

Chuckling, Emma turned, then almost stumbled back over the coffee table when someone shoved her aside. Maya caught her by the arm as the man from earlier stomped on toward the kitchen.

"You might want to change the settings on your *phone*, Frank!" Maya joked.

The man shouted back over his shoulder, "Why? It's not even on."

Everyone around them laughed and returned to their conversations. "Who the hell *is* that?" Emma muttered.

"That's Melinda's husband." Chloe pointed her fork at Emma. "So back off! He's already taken!"

Emma felt several pairs of eyes staring at her. She couldn't tell whether Chloe was trying to be funny, so she forced herself to give her a thumbs-up and pick up some truffle fries while everyone else turned back to Rachelle, who was peppering Maya with questions. "Did they make you squeeze out a tube of toothpaste for your test?"

"Nope! They put me in a room with a dozen five-year-olds for an hour and watched me through a two-way mirror." Maya shrugged, but she was laughing. "I don't even know what I did to pass, but I wasn't about to complain!"

"Ta-*ta*!" Adrianna was at the door, waving outside. She closed it and skipped toward the kitchen, linking arms with another pregnant guest along the way.

A couple with glasses of Prosecco in hand nudged between Emma and Maya to ask something Elsa- and/or Ariel-related. Everyone around Emma was distracted by someone else. There was a small gathering by the door as people retrieved their coats from the closet. Step by step, Emma inched away from the group until she stood alone. This was her chance to escape. She headed for the kitchen, but as the room was emptier now, she could still hear Rachelle, now ranting to someone else:

"Like, what's with the 'crumpled paper' test? Is it supposed to mean something?"

"Who knows? I didn't get that one, either."

"Ugh. 'Geniuses of the world,' my ass. I swear, it's just designed it to work against us."

"But … some of the think-tank team is from Norway, aren't they? So, there were at least a *couple* who helped design the test."

"Whatever. They were obviously in the minority, so I wouldn't be surprised if —"

"Hey," Emma said firmly when she reached Adrianna, ignoring the shock on her and her friend's faces at being interrupted. "I'm going to call it a night."

"*Why?*" Adrianna turned to her, fully concerned now. "You just got here! And there's someone you seriously have to meet — oh, for fuck's sake, don't tell me Hannah left already …"

Emma didn't bother trying to follow Adrianna's gaze around the room. "Why did you invite me to this?" she asked instead.

"I … well, it's been so long since I've seen you." Adrianna's voice went up. "And then Grace mentioned running into you, and I know so many people have questions these days … friends of *mine*, especially … so when Grace said you might have some insight —"

"You thought I could help people pass the *test*?"

"Well, yeah." Adrianna looked ashamed now. "Plus, I haven't seen you in ages! I thought you might like to hang out with people instead of musty old books for a change."

"What makes you think I don't hang out with people?" Emma didn't, not really, but she kept that to herself.

"Well, how the hell would I know? I mean, I haven't seen you on any socials in decades. I know nothing about you, now! It's lucky Grace even ran into you and linked us up. And how often do you go to parties where you can eat stuff from FCBO?" Adrianna gave her a haughty smirk, trying to be funny. "I don't see any *other* librarians getting permits to eat like this, do you?"

Emma looked Adrianna dead in her eye. "You're right," she said after a beat. "You clearly know nothing about me."

Later, Emma would never be certain how it happened: she knew she was ready to leave. She knew she wanted to use the bathroom before she left. She knew she wanted to at least try a bit of castella before leaving too. The sequence and order of priorities would fluctuate in her memory for years. What Emma did know was that someone stepped right in between them, distracting Adrianna entirely with questions about the Prosecco and how much the food permit must have cost for the party.

The rest of it would forever be a blur of images, but the final frame would always remain the same, with Emma in the bathroom, the door locked, her fork in one hand, and the plate of imported Japanese cake gripped firmly in the other.

The fork sank down easier than Emma had anticipated. That made sense — although it looked like her dish sponges at home, it was still cake. Not that she'd tried to slice those sponges. She hadn't reached that stage, yet.

Emma lifted the first slice to eye level. It looked like your everyday cake. It smelled light and fragrant. She brought the fork to her mouth and placed the slice on her tongue.

Emma felt the joints in her knees disintegrate.

It wasn't good. It wasn't amazing. It was phenomenal.

Legs weak, she slid down the door until she was sitting on the floor in a heap of happiness. With a satisfied groan, she lifted forkful after forkful of the yellow sponginess to her mouth as she took in her surroundings: the collection of vegan makeup along the shelves. The little corgis in various poses on the shower curtain. The seashells on the toilet. The absence of clean hand towels. Emma absorbed the details around her without judgment or deep reflections. She couldn't even hear the party anymore. The cake had transported her to a secret, silent dimension where the only thing there was to do was chew, swallow, and enjoy.

It felt like comfort. It tasted like time.

And that was all Emma had. She had no idea how long she spent in the bathroom, carving those tiny slices and consuming the castella little by little. She was shocked when she brought her fork down and cut through air. There was none left to eat.

No regrets, though. Not a single one.

Above Emma's head, the doorknob rattled violently. "Someone's in here," she called out, barely recognizing her own sleepy voice.

The doorknob stopped, then rattled again, harder.

"It's *locked*," Emma said, but struggled to her hands and knees to stand up anyway. *Must be one hell of a bathroom emergency*, she thought.

She had just placed the empty cake platter on the counter to pull herself up when the impatient person on the other side of the door proceeded to pound on it.

"What in the hell —?"

Emma had cracked the door open only an inch when the man with the smartphone glasses burst in. He was blocking her now. She couldn't leave the bathroom if she tried.

"What is *that*?"

Emma had no idea where he was even looking. "What?"

He pointed at the plate next to the sink. "*That*. That used to be full. Full of cake. At least two thousand calories." He folded his arms. "That's against the law."

"Uh …" Emma wondered why he didn't seem to need the bathroom so badly anymore.

"I could call the police, you know. Half the women here need food more than you do. My wife needed that cake more than you did." He smirked. Even through his glasses Emma could sense the condescension in his eyes. "In fact ... yeah. I *should* call the police."

Emma had had enough. She didn't need this. It made sense now, how he'd been pushing her all night, and why. She didn't need *any* of it.

The man raised a hand to his temple as Emma, with a smirk of her own, reached for her turtleneck and pulled the collar down, hard, exposing the top of her sternum.

"And tell them what?" she asked.

"Uh —"

Emma brimmed with confidence (and, in all likelihood, the sugar rush from all that cake). *"And tell them what?"* she asked, louder.

The man continued to gape at her in silence. Emma swore she saw the whites of his eyes through his phone, now.

Her smile softened. "That's what I thought."

She wanted to elbow the man out of her way, but she stopped herself. With confident flair, she picked up the plate and handed it to him. He looked down and took it. *Another grenade in kerosene*, Emma thought.

"Excuse me."

The man now seemed to remember Emma was standing there. He jolted, but indeed moved over enough so she could strut out of the bathroom. She swerved around the woman who had just rounded the corner, who was now glaring into the bathroom, yelling, "Frank? What the *hell*?"

She wove through the remaining guests and headed for the closet by the front door. As soon as she located her coat, she saw herself out, putting several buildings between herself and Adrianna's place before she manoeuvred her coat around her body.

Waddling down the rest of the hydrocar-lined street, she promised she'd have a helping of the spinach smoothie sitting in her fridge … no, on second thought, she'd have a nice big one, first thing in the morning. Emma knew she needed all the folate she could get, but tonight, she was too full for anything else.

NOVEL SUGGESTIONS FOR SOCIAL OCCASIONS

Ji Hong Sayo

T wo hundred years after the great fourohfour made the last city uninhabitable, few relics remain. What texts have survived are holy writ; one such sacred book is Paul Pierce's *Novel Suggestions for Social Occasions*, with certain modifications that allow for the new demands of life on the wasteland.

To the Aristocracy of the Wastes
To that much abused, but very eminent class, the society women of the sprawling wastes, this book is dedicated. It is with a realization that they constitute the better half of the best aristocracy in the world — the only real aristocracy in the present day. It is an aristocracy of real merit, entry to which is attained by bone and flint, not by mere

inheritance. No titles are inherited there; they are bought with the hearts of one's enemies. It is an aristocracy of the fittest, not of chance birth. Out of strife is growing a higher and higher standard for each successive generation, and hence it is an aristocracy of ascent and not descent.

Suppers are the favourite social function of wasteland aristocrats. Hence it is with the highest esteem of their station, and the honour they reflect on the land, that this humble volume is recommended to their especial protection and favour.

Harriet pressed a hand down hard over the left side of her petticoat and gave the trickling blood a stern look. She was crouched behind the overturned dinner table, surrounded by cactus crab shells and apple tarts. Clara King knelt beside her, reduced to tears — the gash in her shoulder was one thing, but having a party so thoroughly ruined had discomposed her completely. Mr. Grover might have been useful in this circumstance, but he was bleeding out on the other side of the table. Meanwhile, the four Lucases each carried a garish stone-head axe, as was the fashion in the eastern marsh. They seemed unwilling to rush the barricade, but cowardice would hold them only a moment.

Supper had started well enough, but what else could have been expected when Clara insisted on inviting the Lucases?

They had been celebrating Clara's recent engagement to Mr. Grover, which secured the survival of the House of King, and were to feast on the spoils of the raid that had been run on the

Eltons as an early marriage celebration. The Lucases, being Mr. Grover's cousins, had all but invited themselves, and Clara had not the heart to refuse them. They'd sat down two hours past twilight (the time was called eight o'clock, although the last clock had stopped ticking fifty years prior).

The two Lucas daughters were handsome, rich, idle, and insolent. Though Harriet was the person of the party of highest standing, having led the raid and taken the enemy leader's head, Vera Lucas had wasted no time in growing insolently familiar over brain fritters and chicory-root tea.

"My dear Harriet," she'd said, "will you be on the warrior's pilgrimage many years more? Wandering conquest is honourable to be sure, but so hard on the skin."

"I imagine a few more years, at least."

"That *is* a shame. No one can doubt your skill in battle, of course, but the open wastes give so little opportunity for developing certain varieties of elegance, to say nothing of finding an establishment."

"I thank you for your concern, Miss Lucas, but I'm afraid I am a woman of few talents. I cannot cover screens like Clara, and I fall into a malaise after too many good suppers. In all honesty, my hand is steady only when it holds a weapon." Here Harriet glanced at Mrs. Lucas, who had been the mighty "Mountainous Greta" before her marriage and subsequent decay into blank insensibility. "I don't imagine I'll ever return home but to die, and I hope you'll forgive me for deferring that fate a few years longer."

Clara looked somewhat annoyed by this speech, and Ms. Lucas did not raise the issue again. The tea was attended to in silence, and the party turned to honeyed cakes, a symbol of their victory in burning the Eltons' granary. The cakes were seasoned with nutmeg and served on the bones of the enemy leaders. Harriet took one with careful ritual, laying a gloved hand beside the platter and raising the cake with three fingers, paying homage to worthy enemies. Despite her leadership, the number of casualties had been almost equal on both sides, and her hip still burned where Rodger Elton had grazed her with a club.

Alecia Lucas, the youngest of the party, blithely grabbed three cakes and flicked a hand over the serving dish. "This is Rodger's femur, is it?"

Harriet nearly lost her countenance. To think of calling Mr. Elton "Rodger"! Such presumption and crass familiarity, and not even from the warrior who'd brought him down, which might have been overlooked.

Harriet waited for one of the elder Lucases to reprimand her, but Mr. Lucas looked perfectly pleased with his daughter's liveliness, and Mrs. Lucas's powers of penetration had been so dulled by anaesthetic mushrooms that she was as likely to scold the cakes as her daughters. Though burning with indignation, Harriet calmed herself by discreetly squeezing her knives under the table, and the appetizers were cleared without further incident. The trouble really began, as it so often does, over the devilled cactus crabs.

The wise hostess will be a fount of sparkling conversation during the key transitions in a supper. Dishes served immediately before the main course are to be light, intended to cleanse the palate and whet the appetite. Rare waste mushrooms will serve, as will fertilized lizard eggs, grilled lightly on the skewer. One wishes, at this point, to avoid heavy sauces, which will detract from the main course. Devilling, particularly, may put one's guests in a sullen mood.

The elder Miss Lucas, having taken it into her head to embarrass Harriet, had been waiting for a lull in the conversation, and found her opening while their hostess was sighing to her fiancé.

"Pray, Harriet, would you tell us how you came by that rather substantial scar over your left eye?"

Harriet blushed. Discussing scars was not unknown as an evening game, but was normally played only between intimate friends, in the quiet of the datura parlour. And the long, hypertrophic scar that crawled over her left eye was a far cry from the dainty dart-scratches expected of a society woman.

"Surely we would not wish to distress our friends with stories of blood and smoke, Miss Lucas. Let us talk of the cactus crabs instead. I for one haven't seen such a plump, well-seasoned specimen in years."

Vera Lucas gave a raucous laugh. "Ah, I suppose you don't want to talk of a past embarrassment! Just as well, dear Harriet. Let us discuss our appetizers, and overlook your mediocrity as a raider."

Too late, Clara heard the tone of the conversation and gave Harriet an alarmed look.

For Harriet's part, she had had quite enough of the eldest Lucas daughter and answered her in a cool voice: "Miss Lucas, I earned this scar in fair combat with a worm farmer in Jonestown, past the Southern plateau. His tribe attacked my party while I was unarmed, and slaughtered my fellows — this scar was given before I could reach my spear. Now he is dead, and in that he is joined by his father, his five sons, his four wives, the three men he ran with, and one wretched servant who came at me with a ladle. I mounted their heads with salvia and orange lilies along the roadside, as an offering to my fallen companions. Now, if you wish to be quiet, we can enjoy this delightful supper. If you would instead meet me in a duel with bone and flint, we may at least entertain the rest of our party. The choice of amusements I leave to you, dear Vera."

This had been an honourable challenge to single combat — while it was certainly irregular to issue a challenge before the main course was served, it wouldn't have been improper to duel, with Clara's approval. Harriet was only faintly surprised when the treacherous Vera Lucas instead drew her battle-axe and was joined by her sister and mother.

Harriet had flipped the rough-chipped wooden table, sending Clara's dainty mustard service flying. The Lucases closed ranks around their eldest daughter, Mr. Lucas thundering about reparations and slander, while Mrs. Lucas's eyes cleared and she drew a hidden blowgun from her skirts. Clara had caught a glancing blow to the shoulder, and Mr. Grover, whose gallantry exceeded his competence, had jumped from cover in anger.

His blood was now seeping under the table, and Harriet could but grit her teeth at the thought of it staining her only white dress. Harriet, to maintain decorum, had come armed as lightly as a lady might be: three small bone knives, and not even her leather armour. That left two alive on Harriet's side, and not even a single knife for each enemy. She'd seen worse odds.

Grasping Clara's hands (luckily, she had not lost her gloves in the tumult), Harriet put a flinty edge in her voice: "The armoury-kitchen is at our back. I'll create an opening, and we'll run deeper into the house."

Clara was too oppressed to answer, but she gave a nod. Harriet had raided at Clara's side all through childhood — having gained the King fortune and lost her application, her oldest friend had long since surpassed her in accomplishments, but Clara had the sense not to resent Harriet for her own deficiencies, just as Harriet had never begrudged Clara her fortune. She knew to follow Harriet's orders once blood had been spilled, as surely as Harriet followed hers in the province of directing a household.

Clara held tight to her hand while Harriet braced up against the wall and kicked the table toward their attackers. Harriet stood then, and in the same breath threw a slender shard of bone through Mrs. Lucas's left eye.

> A lady prizes delicacy above all else. Death and dishonour may come, the vital blood may flow, but she shall maintain elegance through all three trials. A dish is to be as dainty and balanced in seasoning as a weapon is balanced in the hand.

The two retreated through the corridor. Out of the corner of her eye, Harriet saw Mrs. Lucas staggered but not downed, her remaining eye blazing, and was tempted to resort to indelicate words. She'd chosen her target carefully: Mountainous Greta had earned her reputation by ripping a raider in half with her bare hands.

Clara stopped at the threshold of the kitchen with Harriet. Her eyes were clear, and she wiped the blood from her shoulder. Harriet gathered a handful of powdered green peppercorns a panicked servant had spilled on the floor.

"It's best you run now, Clara. I'll hold them here."

"I wouldn't hear of it. You're injured and must not risk a fever by overexertion. Besides, it would disgrace my reputation as a hostess if I didn't fight to the last."

Harriet had no time to argue — Mr. Lucas came charging through, and Harriet practised the virtue of economy by throwing a cloud of pepper into his face, saving a knife. Mr. Lucas fell to the ground howling, eyes filled with powdered peppercorns, and the youngest Lucas tripped over him as she followed. Mr. Lucas reached blindly for Harriet's ankle — now *that* would indeed have been an unforgivable breach of etiquette — and Harriet answered with an eloquent kick to his occipital bone, before retreating toward the Pantry.

> When you next are offering an enemy's heart
> in victory, consider the left and right cham-
> bers — the armoury and the kitchen must
> be similarly close, similarly inseparable. As a
> related note to the curious hostess, an ene-
> my heart is best eaten raw (not for the more
> delicate stomach, of course!), and daintily
> garnished with either parsley or waste-truffle,
> but never pepper, which adds astringency.

The two reached the Pantry, the very heart of the King estate, and slammed the wooden door, bolting it with a great wooden beam — even with their axes, the door would hold the Lucases a few minutes. Clara gasped while Harriet drew steady, quick breaths and moved through the drying herbs toward a stock of fire-hardened spears.

> When entertaining, as when in the sight of
> enemies, a lady must never show fatigue. To
> do so invites gossip and arrowheads.

Harriet balanced a spear in her hands, ignoring the clatter of axes on the door, but Clara stayed her hand.

"Wait — wait, my dearest friend. The House of King stands beside you today."

Breath steadier, Clara bent down and opened a heavy chest and, pushing aside the fine coyote skins and dried jasmine that filled it, drew forth the sword of the House of King.

Harriet's breath hitched in her throat. Artifacts of steel had almost all been lost to rust, and the few that remained had long been made useless with use. But the sword of King was fine and dark, shining like lacquered ebony, a hexagonal bar with no cutting edge and no grip, for the conjurers of the time before were inscrutable. Both ends forked and tapered into thin, sharp edges, one a gentle curve, the other bending inward like a fish hook.

"Clara — I couldn't possibly —"

"Silence. This is a solemn moment. This is a sacred weapon, carved before the great fourohfour, crafted by magic long since lost. Its secret name is Raven-Barr; so did its crafters name it. I bind it to you, Harriet Jenkinson of Downsbridge. May you wield it with elegant fury, until your vital blood flows beneath the stars and a lady of greater refinement takes it from you."

Harriet pressed her hand to her mouth. She no longer cried, had finished with it when she buried her brother with a thousand blue hyacinths. But now her tears flowed freely as she knelt and accepted the Raven-Barr, its weight true in her hands. Clara gave her a slight smile.

"The household of King is ruined, dear Harriet. I can't be much more than a liability, but might our old friendship convince you to take an apprentice in your raiding party?"

"It would be my honour."

A dart sliced through the air and sank into Clara's side. She let out a single breath and clasped Harriet's hand, then fell. The three Lucas women had used their axes to hollow a small hole in the door, and Mrs. Lucas still had her blowgun. Harriet whirled on the door. To bring poisoned darts to supper was beyond disgrace — unacceptable in polished society.

She shattered the blowgun and threw back the door, teeth bared in a battle-grimace.

"Come now! I kill no ladies today, only unprincipled swine!"

Vera Lucas rushed in, overeager from hurt pride. Harriet batted her axe aside, shattering the stone head against the Raven-Barr, then countered with a swing to Miss Lucas's head. Her brains soaked the bags of pastry flour. Alecia Lucas still held the shattered remains of the blowgun and was staring at what remained of her sister.

Without pause, Harriet pushed the slightly curving edge of the sword through her chest, twisting to ensure the heart would rupture.

And then there was only the towering Mrs. Lucas, Mountainous Greta, with an axe in either hand and a blaze like the midday sun in her one eye.

"Have no fear, Mrs. Lucas. You'll not be out of your daughters' company long."

At this, Mrs. Lucas unhinged her jaw and howled. Harriet had seen the battle-madness before, from those who returned to that one battlefield whenever blood was spilled. Judicious use of waste mushrooms often heightened the effect.

"No lady surrenders to madness," said Harriet. "Allow me to do a favour for the reputation of Lucas Manor."

She swung her sword harder than she'd have dared swing an ordinary wooden weapon, and Mrs. Lucas caught the blow on her axe's handle, which splintered as she did. The other axe came down hard and Harriet rolled to avoid it, swinging at Mrs. Lucas's good leg. She felt the bone go, but Mrs. Lucas did not fall, merely shifted her weight as she brought her axe in a wide arc, drawing blood from Harriet's cheek.

Before she could recover her footing, Harriet was driven back to the wall, staggering under the weight of Mrs. Lucas's blows. Mrs. Lucas charged and brought down both axes with skull-breaking strength. Harriet fell, as they did — fell between Mrs. Lucas's legs. The Raven-Barr she left wedged between Mrs. Lucas and the wall, the force of Mrs. Lucas's charge driving its gently curved end through her abdomen and clean out her back.

Mrs. Lucas turned and tried to raise her axes again, but brought them no higher than her elbow.

Harriet looked at her calmly. "All the mushrooms on the waste won't help a pierced diaphragm. You have a handful of breaths left to you."

Harriet stepped forward, grasped the sword, and slammed her head into Mrs. Lucas's nose. At last she fell, unbreathing.

After checking that none of her opponents still drew breath, and finishing Mr. Lucas, who was trying to wash his eyes in potato water, Harriet returned to Clara.

There were no parting words — lichen-slug venom paralyzed the mouth too quickly. But Harriet laid a hand on her friend's arm and rested with her till her ragged gasps slowed.

"You entertained as well as any society lady could hope, my Clara."

At this, the gasps stopped.

———————

Harriet Jenkinson of Downsbridge left her last friend's house with the pyre still burning, and walked toward Lucas Manor. All that remains of the manor today is ash and pink carnations. Now, they whisper stories of Lady Raven-Barr, the eater of many hearts, and raiders burn their *own* houses when she draws near, hoping to avoid her wrath. Her legend has even been added to that most sacred of texts, and her legacy secured for as long as elegant society survives in the waste.

> Aspiring entertainers should keep in the fore-
> front of their minds the wise advice of one
> Harriet Jenkinson, a lady of refinement if ever
> there was one:
> "The success, or lack thereof, of a supper is
> largely determined when the guest list has been
> made. And one must never devil cactus crabs."

JUST A TASTE

A.G.A. Wilmot

Orion's three o'clock, Eliseo de Luca, appeared above her suddenly, towering and cast in shadow like a skyscraper silhouetted against the sun. She didn't hear him arrive, didn't even notice when he opened the door and stealthed inside, very phantom-esque. She looked up, locked eyes with him as he lowered himself, smooth like honey off the edge of a spoon, into the brown-leather seat on the other side of her glass desk. Unbuttoned his grey suit jacket — *silk*, she thought, recalling what she'd gleaned from the dossier compiled by Xyla in admin: old money, skins in reserve, and off-the-book halos backed up at myriad server farms around the planet — and ran his hand through his short, black-and-grey hair before he draped one arm over the back of the chair as if he owned the place.

"I want a burger," he stated firmly, without hesitation or introduction. "Not some impossible I-can't-believe-it's-not-cow bullshit. I want to know that taste for real. I want the clearest shard you can dredge up, and I want it front of mind. Now."

Orion was taken aback at his forward nature. *A man who has never heard the word "no,"* she thought to herself.

"I think that can be arranged." She leaned back in her seat and tented her fingers. "It's safe to assume, then, you don't have any potential donors who might assist you in this matter?"

"Wouldn't be here if I did."

"Of course." She sat up straight and swept one hand across the dormant display inset into her desk, which immediately hummed to life. A holographic screen appeared between them, projected up from the surface. Orion pulled up several files, images, and data, not unlike a restaurant menu. "We have many different approach vectors at our disposal. You choose the meat — cow, bison, kangaroo — and how you'd like it prepared, and the desired bun and condiments, and I can help design for you a culinary experience like no oth—"

"No."

Orion paused. She shifted her gaze. He was staring at her through the display, eyes radiating a threatening kind of confidence.

"I'm sorry?" she said.

"I don't want some … synthetic dream facsimile. I want a *real* burger. A mess of one, bloody, straight off a grill somewhere. The real thing. And I want you to get it for me."

Orion lowered an open palm and the display vanished. "Mister de Luca, that's —"

"You're going to tell me it's not possible," he said, uncrossing and recrossing his legs. "And I'm going to tell you I don't care."

"Mister de Luca," Orion said again, clasping her hands together, "we design memories here. That's what we do at Ephemera. I can make for you the experience of your choosing, but — much as I wish I could — I cannot do what you're asking."

"As a designer, no, of course not. But as a scrubber ..." He glared knowingly.

Orion remained steadfast, emotionless. She worried her knees might give out if she were to try and stand. "I —"

"Know exactly what I'm talking about." He tossed something small and round onto her desk. It was a thin ring no more than a few centimetres in diameter, plastic with visible circuitry throughout and a gap at one end. It was speckled in spots — red and dried. Extracted not too long ago, she realized.

"My stepbrother," he stated dispassionately. "You did some work for him. Don't deny it," he said when he saw Orion open her mouth to speak. "He was quite clear about the memories you gave him. My wife's, if I'm not mistaken. I'm not sure how you got them — there are hours missing from her memory — but, obviously, you have talent." He paused. "It's a shame, really. Had he gone after a different account, I might not have noticed the missing funds. But Marcello never did learn how to hide his tracks."

Orion swallowed nervously. "You're not police, then."

The man laughed, short and punctuated.

"And all you want ... is a burger."

"You assume vengeance?"

"Many in your position —"

"I assure you, Miss Lovatt, there are very few in my position." He uncrossed his legs and leaned forward, his stare softening somewhat. "I want for very little these days. There's not much I can't buy for myself, materially speaking. Experiences, however ... Certain rarities require more effort, and outside assistance. For which, again, I am very willing to pay. You did my brother a service. It was an empty, dispassionate transaction — I know this, regardless of its cost. I do not seek retribution for this, but I do desire your skill."

Orion grew increasingly aware of the small size of her office. Of the darkened windows, the privacy they afforded their clients.

How closed off she was, suddenly. Alone. At this man's mercy.

"I want a burger, Miss Lovatt. A real one. I want to know that taste for myself." He sat back again, grinned disarmingly. "And I want you to crack open a Legacy and get it for me."

———

"For real? He said 'crack open a Legacy'?"

Orion nodded as she finished drying her long, red hair. She glanced across the living room to Zac, engrossed in messages pinging his Ocular. *Probably John*, she thought. The two had been attached at the hip for months now.

Zac had tried to convince her to go with him when he got his Ocular installed, but she found the idea repellent. Not so much the procedure itself — having a slim tract of circuitry fastened to the side of one's eyeball — as the risk to one's privacy. She saw enough from inside the minds of others; she didn't need to open up her own brain to additional security breaches.

"So ... what're you going to do?"

She stopped and stared, damp towel in her lap. "What do you mean?"

"Do you need to pack, contact Gregor, and get an ID swap?"

"No?" she said, slightly confused. "Zac, I took the job."

He sat up and tapped the side of his head, and Orion saw the faint digital readout vanish from across his left eye. "You did what now?"

"He knew who I was. He has money, connections … If I try to disappear, I won't get far. I know this. He knows it too."

"What's the play, then?"

She shrugged. The bathrobe was starting to itch — one of them needed to do laundry before the heat death of the universe. "Like he said: I need to find a Legacy."

Zac scoffed. "Good fucking luck. It's hard enough finding a synth who remembers what cows even looked like, let alone how they tasted. And anyone that ancient likely has an uncrackable safe for a mind."

Loath though she was to admit it, Zac had a point. Going after a Legacy was a different sport entirely. Most halos she scrubbed were unclaimed bodies — people with maybe one, two backup skins, and that was all they could afford. They'd get a good couple of hundred years or more if they played it safe, took care of themselves. Not like Legacies — those who could afford and store backed-up bodies and endless halos on vast servers, ensuring some modicum of artificial immortality.

"I have to try," she said. "I don't think failure is an option here."

Zac shook his head. "All this for a dead thing."

"No," she said. "All this for a memory."

———

It had been predicted, more than two centuries prior, that an out-of-control population crisis would one day spell the end of fresh meat.

Plagues, however, like to slide onstage off cue and on their own timetable, and fuck everything up. And with the last cow having died — victims, all, of a bovine flu that had swept the planet long before Orion's grandparents had even been born — finding a concise memory of that taste, that very specific experience, would be like searching for a needle in a warehouse of haystacks.

Fortunately, Orion had a magnet.

Their name was Marrow. They were a Legacy of a different sort. They hadn't achieved anything great; nor were they born into wealth. No, Marrow was a life-thief. They'd copied and fixed and resoldered versions of their own halo more times than they could count; they'd slipped into every unclaimed skin they could bargain or barter for from the backs of rebirthing clinics desperate to offload bodies whose owners had lapsed in their storage payments.

They were a chimera — a being of no static appearance, an honest-to-God amalgam of different lives. This was true, too, of their mind, which they'd fitted with every rare or unconventional experience that had crossed their path. Well, those they couldn't sell.

Orion knew Marrow through necessity — they ran a side hustle as proprietor of an underground memory-trading ring, which was how most freelance scrubbers survived, pulling memories from cloned or unclaimed halos and repurposing them for public use. Certainly Orion would have preferred to find employment with a legit rebirthing centre, helping the newly dead by honouring their memoriams: taking their halos and digging into them, teasing apart unwanted memories — how they died, various hurts caused and levied against — and suturing everything together again, to minimize the gaps as much as possible before the start of their next life. But competition outweighed demand, and such appointments were difficult to come by. Thus, Orion satisfied her needs through other means, by stealing, copying, and splicing what she could — and sometimes what she was hired to find. Which was how she'd come to be on Eliseo de Luca's radar in the first place.

Through Marrow, Eliseo's stepbrother, Marcello, had come to her, sobbing about how his evil older brother had stolen from him, and how Eliseo's wife was the key to it all — how the younger Marcello could regain his supposedly lost fortunes if only they could pilfer her memories. In the end, Orion hadn't cared whether Marcello was telling the truth so long as he was willing — and able — to pay. It had been a challenge, that was what had appealed most. Orion's day job, writing artificial dreams and memories at Ephemera, afforded her some modicum of creative satisfaction, but the experiences were too slight for her liking. Too unreal, too lost in the uncanny valley. There was simply no substitute for seeing and experiencing a real memory for yourself — something personal, something impossible or unheard of.

Something long lost to time.

———

Late that same night, not long after Zac had disappeared into his room, Orion put on her black hoodie, grabbed her black messenger bag filled with her gear, and slipped out of the midtown Toronto apartment they shared. She made her way through the quiet Wednesday-at-2:00-a.m. streets to one of the decommissioned subway entrances a fifteen-minute walk away and descended, careful to avoid the drunks on the steps — and at least one poor bastard lying in a pool of blood with a ragged, gaping hole in the back of his neck where someone had stolen his halo not five minutes earlier. At the bottom, she vaulted effortlessly over the rusted-in-place turnstile and went down to the train platform, and through a service access door half a kilometre down the southbound tunnel.

The inside of the tunnel was commotion bathed in red and purple and black, an underground community where it was difficult to get a clear look at anyone. Orion pulled her hood over her head and kept her eyes to the ground as she slipped between bodies huddled close around sellers' tables displaying halos, like sidewalk vendors hocking cheap jewellery to travellers and passersby. Most were unlabelled, their memories taken as a whole, like an extremely personal and private blind box — purchasers picked them on a whim, trusting individual sellers with whom they'd dealt before. Many, including some scrubbers, bought in bulk and dissected the halos on their own, taking individual memories and copying them to shards before turning around and selling them to people searching for something new — something they never would have experienced for themselves. The digitally transferred memories rarely fit cohesively within another's mind, but for those willing to go this route, that wasn't a concern. The point, simply, was to experience something new — however "experience" was defined.

She made her way to a larger booth near the back of the market, down a flight of metal stairs and surrounded by heavy piping and electrical. Inside was a person with dishevelled brown-and-grey hair, a weeks-unkempt beard, and a gaunt frame encased in dry, parchment-like skin. Track marks up and down each arm. "What's the point of living all these lives if we don't live them to the goddamn fullest?" Marrow had said to her once, when she came upon them with a needle still in their arm. They'd OD'd seven times in the five years Marrow and Orion had known one another, and every time appeared to her again in a new and unfamiliar body, ready for another round of targeted self-destruction. The chimera knew every mortician, every rebirth tech in town — whenever Marrow wound up on a slab, the second their halo was identified, they were extracted and whisked away, fitted with whatever was on the rack, with the full knowledge they were good for it; they'd make sure that whoever helped them got first pick of any choice memories that came their way.

Orion wasn't as well known a commodity, but she had regular interactions with four or five morticians' offices throughout town and was usually among the first called when a fresh corpse rolled in. She'd go in, clone what she could, and disappear with few words spoken between them. Whatever she found of note, whatever seemed especially unique or worthwhile — travel to exotic locales, sunset dances on rooftops, climbs to the peaks of the world's tallest mountains — she copied to individually labelled shards and brought to Marrow, who paid her up front and paid handsomely.

Rarely did she try and purchase memories, but this was indeed a rare situation. She'd gotten in over her head with the de Luca family without realizing. She shouldn't have asked her bartender friend, Gemma, to drug Eliseo's wife that night so Orion could scan and clone her halo, using needle insertion through a microscopic hole in her neck that she wouldn't feel or remember an hour after waking up. But Orion had, and now she was paying for it.

Marrow raised their head in a drugged stupor as Orion made her way downstairs. "The prodigal daughter returns!" they said jovially.

"Hey, Mare," she said, keeping her distance.

They clambered to their feet, using the nearby wall to steady themselves. They were looking especially meth-chic, Orion thought to herself — blackened tombstone teeth and deep hollows under both eyes.

They grinned. "What wondrous things have you brought me today?"

Orion fished a half-dozen shards from the messenger bag slung across her chest. She passed them to Marrow, who stared at the slender, translucent, postage-stamp-sized bits of plastic in their palm, as if at seeds they expected to take root and grow.

"Couple of weddings — real fancy ones, expensive. One skydiving, uh, *incident*, and the life and times of two actors."

"Film?"

"Stage."

Marrow let out a sound like a wet fart. "Those don't sell, and you know it."

"They do — you just gotta know how to sell them."

"Collectors? Critics?"

"Acting students. Understudies."

"Narcissists in training."

Marrow exhaled, and Orion fought the urge to cringe at the death of their breath. They passed her a roll of bills then. She clutched it tight but remained in place.

"Something else on your mind?" Marrow said.

Orion cleared her throat. "I need a memory. Clear as possible."

"For yourself, or ..."

"For a client."

"I see." They leaned back, arms folded. "And what, pray tell, is this client seeking?"

"The taste of beef. They want a burger."

Marrow snort-laughed. "Oh, is that all?"

"That's it — just a burger."

"Right, just a burger. Sure they don't want to also walk on-stage with Springsteen? Act in a Spielberg film? Read the first draft of a Nabokov?" They shook their head. "Just a burger, Christ ..."

"You don't have it, then."

"No, I don't fucking have a fucking burger. Ain't no one around even old enough to remember what that tastes like."

"There are," she said. "You and I both know that."

"Yeah, and unless you've got an 'in' with a Legacy, you ain't getting at them. You know what they do with their memories? They keep them. Maybe they pass a few to their idiot kids or something, but that's it. You find a shard from a Legacy down here, you've got yourselves a murder."

Orion sighed. "Shit."

Marrow glared at her, eyes narrowed. "This isn't just a pay-day for you, is it?"

She met their stare.

"I want a burger, Miss Lovatt. A real one. I want to know that taste for myself. And I want you to crack open a Legacy and get it for me."

"And if I can't?"

Eliseo de Luca leaned forward, eyes like knives. "You will, or I might be forced to reconsider my feelings on vengeance."

"It's my life," she said.

Marrow looked away. "That's ... real tough shit, kiddo. Wish I could help."

"Can't you?"

"I just said I —"

She stepped forward. "Are you telling me, in all those shards you've taken for yourself, all those halos you've torn apart and duct-taped to your own like some weird fucking antique mind collector, not one person in one life has eaten a damn burger?"

Marrow stepped forward in kind. "We're not talking about what's in my head," they said. "Whatever I've got, that's mine. I earned it for myse—"

"You stole it."

"*I earned it,*" they sneered. "You know what? Get out. We're done here."

"Mare, please, if I go back empty handed, he's gonna —"

Marrow leaned forward, face to face. "Not. My. Problem."

Orion watched then as they turned back inside their tented booth, to try and stitch a new life, a new set of memories to their already overwhelmed self, or to go and die again — it didn't matter which. She waited a minute or two to see if they would re-emerge. When they didn't, she returned upstairs to the chaos and death of the memory marketplace.

———

It was nearly dawn when Orion, hidden in the gloom of the subway tunnel, witnessed Marrow's exit from the service access door. They stumbled out, visibly high on whatever new and debilitating cocktail they'd poured into their veins. Orion was just glad she hadn't missed their exit. They were always the last to leave when the market shut down for the night, but it had taken her longer than expected to make the trip to Gemma's and back. She was just lucky Gemma had still been awake, and that she didn't ask questions when Orion said she needed to raid her medical supply cabinet.

Mrs. de Luca wasn't the first time Orion had asked Gemma to run interference — twice she had waited with Gemma outside a mark's residence, ready with a rag and a bottle of chloroform. The two of them went back years, and Orion always made sure to give Gemma a solid cut of whatever she made from the memories they cloned.

"Want me to come with?" Gemma had said, stifling a yawn. She'd arrived home from her late shift only thirty minutes earlier.

"No," Orion said. "This one's mine. But thanks."

Gemma stared at her curiously. "You sure you're okay?"

Orion had stared at the bottle of colourless liquid in her hand. "Yeah," she'd lied. "Everything's under control."

Now, Orion watched from behind a steel girder as Marrow hobbled down the near-silent subway tunnel. She waited for several seconds, to make sure no one was following, and then slipped out from her hiding spot. Silently, she pulled the bottle of chloroform from her bag and unscrewed the cap, then poured a bit of it into a rag Gemma had found under her kitchen sink. Still moving, Orion tried to screw the cap back onto the bottle but dropped it. It hit the pavement like a penny dropping in church.

Marrow spun around like a startled deer. Squinted into the dark. "The fuck? Orion, that you? What're you —"

She lunged. Forced the rag over their mouth and nose. They swiped at her through their haze before, slowly at first and then rather quickly, their arms and legs went limp. Orion carefully moved the rag — Marrow was unconscious.

She looked around the vastness of the empty subway tunnel and realized she had no idea what to do next.

What am I doing what am I doing what the ever-loving fuck am I doing?

Truthfully? Orion had no idea. She'd never attempted such a messy hack — on her knees, just inside the access door to the market, one foot holding it shut while she attempted to thread through the back of Marrow's neck with both hands shaking. Took a breath, two; held them until her heart started to s-l-o-w. She re-upped — hands steadier, she slipped through and blindly found her way to the pinhole-sized access port on the halo fastened between vertebrae of Marrow's cervical spine like she'd done hundreds of times before.

She pulled a tablet from her messenger bag and connected the thread to it, linking Marrow's mind to her device. She was shocked to find they had almost no encryption whatsoever — if they were a "true" Legacy, they would never have been caught without it. They were still unconscious, but they didn't need to be awake for their brain to hear and respond to suggestive prompts.

"Burger," she said, watching the readout on her tablet — an aftermarket program cobbled together from fragments of dream-writing software and shit professional-grade scrubbers employed when wiping fresh trauma from a new-newborn. Onscreen appeared vast lines of code denoting smells, sounds, taste — human sense-memory compressed and converted to a stream of consciousness consisting of billions of algorithmic strands.

"Burger," she said again. "Ground beef." She watched carefully as the readouts changed with every word uttered — as the dreamware hack gradually helped to highlight and isolate common threads among the code: sense-memories specific to her target.

She said it again, adding specific search parameters to help narrow the field: bun, cheese, lettuce, tomato, pickles, mustard, ketchup. Everything she could think of off the menu at a fast-food place that still sold everything but the now-extinct backbone of its enterprise's origins.

The numerical strings onscreen isolated further. Just glancing at the data, Orion was now able to see common threads appearing with greater frequency. She was getting close. Marrow did, in fact, have the memory she was looking for. How they'd gotten it — from what Legacy corpse they managed to come across — she could not fathom. She wondered what else she might glean from them while already inside. Steak tartar? Roast beef? A meatball sandwich?

"Uhhhh ..."

Orion snapped to attention — Marrow was starting to stir.

"Shit," she muttered under her breath.

"What the hellllllll ..." They tried to turn their head.

Panicking, Orion pulled the bottle of chloroform from her bag again. Marrow saw, tried reaching limply for it. She pulled it away and — without thinking — smacked them in the back of the head. They hit the pavement hard and were out cold. Again.

Orion had another problem now. She'd isolated the necessary memory and copied it to her tablet — she'd put it on a shard later, at home — but a new string of numbers was now travelling through Marrow's brain. Synapses firing, building connections, strengthening a new and unshakable memory: Orion. Attack.

She could see it, even if all she could see was code — new strains repeating over and over again, threading through their mind like a serpent, seeding itself deep like only trauma can. If Marrow had any sort of outside server access, she was screwed — their backup would have already received this new info. But if they were purely local, as she suspected, hoped, she could cut and —

Marrow reached out suddenly, grabbed her wrist. Turned their head and growled, "*You.*"

Orion reacted without thinking. She hit them again with the bottle, breaking it over the back of their head with a loud shatter like a rock through plate glass. They weren't knocked out this time, but before they could respond, before she could pause and ask herself what the fuck she was about to do, she took the jagged half of the bottle still in hand and drove it into the back of Marrow's neck. Sawed through skin as they screamed. She pushed their head into the pavement, to muffle their cries, and continued to cut with everything she could until there was a hole in Marrow's neck large enough for her to slip inside with her fingers and a pair of pliers she kept in her bag for emergencies, and extract the halo from Marrow's spine.

Someone who'd been alive as long as Marrow, Orion wasn't sure how much of them was on the halo pinched between her fingers and how much of it had managed to imprint on their grey matter. She couldn't take the risk and, halo in one hand, drove the broken bottle as hard as she could into the hole she'd made, twisting it until Marrow, until their current shell, stopped twitching in kind.

She stood there, in the empty, red-lit marketplace beneath the city, and stared at the dead at her feet and in her hand, and asked herself how it had come to this.

———

Orion thought she would've had longer. She thought if she left without a word, if she emptied out all her accounts and booked the first flight out of town under an alias she'd used early on in her career moonlighting as a memory-thief, she might've made it farther than the other side of the continent, waiting in LAX for a connecting flight to New Zealand, before de Luca's men appeared out of nowhere. They flanked her, ushered her out of the airport and into the back of a black sedan idling just outside. She'd thought, maybe, she had a chance.

"It wouldn't have mattered," de Luca said an hour later, after she was waved into the downtown LA nightclub he apparently owned. Whether he'd been here already on business or flown out from Toronto on the same flight as she, Orion had no way of knowing. For all she knew, de Luca was illegally doubled and existed here, there, potentially everywhere. She'd seen it before — few were strong enough to manage a hive mind connecting multiple bodies, leaving no memories unshared, but she got the impression de Luca was like few others in that regard.

"You could have gone anywhere. I still would have found you."

Orion nodded nervously. "I know."

"Then why run?"

"I ..."

"Killed a Legacy, I know. Not one of our better ones, certainly, but still."

She looked up in horror. "You know?"

De Luca grinned. "You still don't understand, Miss Lovatt." He approached, crouched in front of her, stared up and into her eyes. "Now — did you find what I asked?"

She nodded, clutching her messenger bag, the halo hidden inside a jewellery case that was X-ray proof and, to airport security, would have appeared no different than an extra battery for her tablet.

"I haven't yet put it on a shard, but it's here. I've isolated it."

He cocked his head to one side. "In all that mess of a mind, did you … happen to stumble upon anything else?"

"I … I'm not sure," she said. "There's so much. They —"

"They were a chimera, I know. That's why I asked." De Luca paused. "Do you think, with enough time and the right prompts, you could pull anything more from them?"

"I … Perhaps? Mister de Luca, what're you —"

"I know a great many chefs around this world," he said, standing back up and straightening out his tan suit jacket. "Few, if any, are Legacies. With what's potentially in this mind … You and I, Miss Lovatt, we could give them something thought lost. We could help them *remember* things they themselves have never experienced. They could learn. They could adapt. They could help bring new joy to this world by giving us a taste of what we've lost."

His words were a velvet sheath around a knife — she felt their warmth, their promise, but remained very aware of the danger just beneath the surface.

"I can offer you protection," he said. "If you decide you'd like to work with me on this."

Decide. The word was a splinter in Orion's brain. But …

"I can offer you the chance to help build a legacy of a different sort. For yourself. I can offer you immortality — true immortality. Just a taste, but a taste is more than most people experience in several lifetimes."

Orion clutched her bag to her chest. She imagined returning to her old life, the ever-present threat of Marrow, of what she had done being discovered. She imagined continuing to toil away, writing dreams she didn't believe in by day and swiping memories from corpses by night. And she thought of what de Luca had said — about bringing something back to this world. A flavour on the tongue long lost to time. A communal experience once shared the world over. A taste — of something more, something impossible.

She looked up, met de Luca's stare.

"When do we start?"

RUBBER ROAD

Terri Favro

Chewing gum can fool you into thinking your stomach is full. For two days, Connie and I survived on Dentyne and Orange Crush from an On the Run store at a gas station in Wainfleet, the only stuff left on the shelves. We chewed and rechewed the same giant wads of gum to keep our minds off our hunger pains. At night, we'd stick the big, grey lumps on our saddles and pop them back in our mouths the next morning. Tastes like Dad's oatmeal, Connie said. At least the gum didn't give us the shits, the way Orange Crush did.

In Ridgeway, we coasted to a stop in front of a convenience store with an unbroken front window. Stan's Grocery and Variety. We looked in and saw racks full of chips and Cheezies. My mouth watered so much at the sight of all that salt and fat that I spat out my gum without thinking. When we tried the front door, we found out why the place hadn't been ransacked: a big black-and-tan German shepherd stood on the other side, barking its head off, probably as out of its mind with hunger as we were.

What do we do now? asked Connie.

We wait, I said.

Wait for what?

For the dog to die.

Connie slid down the front of the store and rested her head in her arms. Her skin looked white under the raw patches of sunburn. Malnutrition setting in, I figured. I probably looked just as bad as she did. A diet of gum and soda will do that to you. I had to find real-ish food soon or we'd be too weak to keep moving.

Connie was still fixated on the fucking dog.

Poor thing. We should feed it something.

I looked at my sister in amazement.

What, like our fingers and legs? If we had something to feed it, we'd have eaten it already.

We could try to make friends, she suggested. Show it that we're not going to hurt it.

It's a guard dog. Probably trained to kill, I reminded her.

Funny how we almost never found dogs in the houses where we'd taken shelter, not even ones with BEWARE OF DOG signs. People took their pets with them, knowing they'd never be back, and left their doors unlocked so that maybe refugees could hide in their powder rooms or closets during an onslaught. Stores were a different story. The only way we could get in was to break a window or crawl into places where someone had broken in before us. Vaults would have been a great place to hide, but the banks were always locked up tight. Selfish bastards, that's what I say. More concerned about their useless stacks of money than giving people a shot at survival. They hadn't yet accepted what the rest of us knew: that without blood in your veins, money in your pockets doesn't mean fuck all.

Inside the cardboard box strapped to the back of my bike, Obie meowed and scratched, trying to get out. He didn't like dogs any more than I did. I opened the box and let him have a look around.

The land had been wiped clean of dogs, cats, cows, horses, pretty much every warm-blooded thing, so keeping Obie alive seemed like a smart move. If the mice and rats came back big time, we'd need cats to protect our crops, right? Assuming there would be crops. That's the kind of thing Dad would have said was good thinking. In the meantime, Obie could still hunt up the odd rodent, but they were getting harder and harder to find.

It took a day and a half for the dog's barks to slowly die away. In the meantime we chewed the last of the Dentyne and watched the sky. We were lucky; day after day, we looked up at nothing but puffy clouds, like in the olden times of a month ago. Connie and I slept in the alley behind the store. From time to time, I'd yell and bang on the windows to see if I could rouse the dog. Its barks were getting weaker and weaker. Finally, even with Connie and me yelling and smacking a bike pump against the metal bars of a back window, the dog didn't make a sound.

Let's go, I said.

We used the bike pump to smash in the front window. The dog was inside, curled up in a corner next to an empty bucket — probably where his owners had left him some water. Connie found a towel in a back room and draped it over the dead dog while we ransacked the store. Ripped-up plastic bread bags and pepperoni stick cartons littered the floor. That must have been how the dog stayed alive so long, tearing apart whatever food it could get at. But there was still plenty on the shelves that the dog either wouldn't eat or couldn't get at.

Cheetos. Dehydrated noodles in a cup. Cans of tuna, brown beans, tomato soup — even packets of Pounce and pull-tab cans of Friskies for Obie. We sat on the floor of the store, stuffing ourselves, then started working our way through the freezer, which, to our amazement, was still working, holding unspoiled tubs of ice cream and boxes of Popsicles. Even the AC was running. Stan must have thoughtfully hooked up a generator to make sure his guard dog didn't cook to death inside the store.

Our stomachs tight as drums from all the gorging, we stretched out on the floor to read newspapers dating back about three weeks. One front page had a photograph of a highway jammed with cars, the windshields smashed, bodies pinioned behind deflated airbags. I looked at the photo for a long time, wondering if the person who took it was still alive.

While we digested all the junk food and canned food, I decided to tell Connie about a dream I'd been having. I was sitting across from Mom in our kitchen, the way it looked when Connie and I were little kids: white walls with harvest-gold trim and oak accents. She was drinking lemon tea, her fingers drumming against her favourite china tea mug, printed with the words "Keep Calm." I stared at her fingers gripping the cup, the cuticles all bloody and picked away. Mom always did that when she was nervous, chewing and ripping at her fingers. In the dream, I never looked up from her hands.

When a swarm of moths rose out of Mom's cup, she pinched her nose and pressed her lips together, but she couldn't hold her breath forever. When she finally exhaled, the moths swarmed into her mouth and nostrils, inflating her head like a balloon. After she'd staggered around the kitchen for a few seconds, gurgling and windmilling her arms, she collapsed onto the table in front of me, her head making a deflating sound as it flattened. That was always the point when I woke up.

Through a mouthful of dry noodles, Connie said, Your subconscious is trying to deal with things, Katy.

I didn't say anything, because my subconscious seemed pretty fucking close to just replaying reality.

From under the blanket we heard a sound. A low whine. Obie ran to a corner of the room and hissed.

Oh my God, it's still alive, said Connie.

I sat, looking at her. I knew what was coming.

We can save it.

No, I said.

Come on, Katy.

She started searching the shelves and found a can of Alpo.

With the next onslaught, he's dead, I pointed out. What are you saving its life for?

We could take him along, she said, opening the can with her Swiss Army knife.

Obie doesn't like dogs. Neither do I, I said.

Connie read the dog's name off its collar. "Ernst."

Sounds like a Nazi name, I said. Just your type.

Connie stuck a finger into its muzzle and dripped water onto the edge of its lip. The dog's legs jerked as if it was about to start running.

Poor thing, he's dying of dehydration, Connie said.

Just don't get bit, I reminded her. All we've got is a tube of Polysporin.

Connie grabbed two big bottles of Evian from the cooler and filled the bucket. She grabbed Ernst around his middle and helped him stand on shaky legs to slurp up the water.

By the end of the day, Ernst was eating solid food. He nosed at Obie, who scratched him to show him who was boss. Ernst whined and backed away.

We stayed in the back room of the store with Obie and Ernst for a day. I rummaged under the counters for practical stuff. Band-Aids. Tampax. Tylenol. Hand sanitizer. Wet Wipes. Behind some bleach, I found a Tupperware container full of what looked like sugar. I dabbed a few grains on the tip of my tongue — sweet, but slightly bitter. Same stuff Dad used in the barn: poison mixed with sugar to make it taste good. Rats gobbled it up and bled to death. I figured rat-sugar might come in handy, even if every rat, mouse, and other warm-blooded pest was already sucked dry. There were still cold-blooded vermin out there. I slipped it into my backpack when Connie was having a pee.

When we rode away, Ernst chased us for a few blocks, barking like crazy, then gave up and went back to the store to wait for the owners who would never return. I could hear Connie snuffling on her bike.

My front tire blew outside Port Colborne when I rode over a chunk of jagged glass, probably a broken rear-view mirror that had fallen off one of those asshole-ferrying e-bikes with all their owners' worldly belongings strapped on the back. Most of the asphalt on the trail was broken up and grown over — all it takes is a few weeks without a weed whacker and nature starts running wild. The overgrowth would have looked cool if it hadn't slowed us down.

I braked to a stop as Connie's skinny back disappeared into the distance. *Flat*, I screamed.

Up the trail, Connie turned and looked back at me, her face in shadow, the sick sun behind her; I had this uneasy feeling she was about to keep going because she was pissed with me for abandoning Ernst. After a few seconds, she rode back.

I crouched and ran my thumb over my wheel. I could feel the chunk of mirror embedded in my tire. A pea-sized drop of blood fell from my thumb.

Oh shit, said Connie when she reached me. Can't you just ride on it 'til we get over the border?

I shook my head. We're at least two hours from the Falls and I'll be riding on my rim by then.

Shit, Connie mumbled again, rummaging in her pannier for the patch kit. We don't have time for this.

The sky had turned the colour of lemon tea. Soon it would deepen to a nauseating shade of cat piss.

We have time, I said.

We've got an hour. Maybe two, said Connie, handing me the tube of rubber cement.

Three hours, maybe more, I corrected her.

With her teeth, Connie ripped open the packet holding the patch. We don't know, do we?

The sky had turned from the pale yellow of lemonade to the plastic orange of cheese slices. When that sick yellow cloud changed to ochre, it would be time to take cover. The turkey vultures knew this too. I could see them making lazy circles in the thermals above the gorge. They look nice, at a distance like that, but Connie and I had seen them close up, their ugly heads stuck down in someone's chest cavity. We'd seen them picking through the dusty cadavers all the way along the bike trail. After a while, the cadavers just started reminding us of an overcooked turkey carcass turning to dust.

I held the inner tube while she squeezed a line of rubber cement around the puncture. I wanted to point out that every kilometre we rode to the south meant it took a little longer for the onslaught to catch up with us. Connie hadn't figured that out yet. I didn't want to get into an argument, so she'd just keep her mind on fixing my tire.

Like Mom's cup said: *Keep calm.*

———————

I'd never heard that saying until last year, long before the first onslaught, when Dad gave Mom a gift basket from the Christian Reformed Church Mother's Day Catalogue, containing lavender foot soak, a "clean" romance novel, antioxidant chocolate truffles, and a pink mug printed with the words "KEEP CALM AND WAIT FOR THE RAPTURE." Connie explained to me that the saying was a meme from an ancient war in England: "Keep Calm and Carry On." Meaning, don't freak out under pressure. Stay cool and do what you have to do.

Mom liked to make Lemon Zinger tea in that mug and sit across the kitchen table from me, explaining what a total fuck-up I was. The words "not meeting your potential" and "such a disappointment to Dad and me" and "after what happened to your sister, we'd hoped that at least you'd turn out okay" came up a lot. I just kept my eyes on Mom's nail-bitten fingers tapping the words "KEEP CALM."

The last time we had one of our little talks was when Mom's biggest problem was still just me. She didn't like it that I didn't care about school, that my biggest ambition was to keep calm and carry on, living on our farm with Connie and Obie, our twelve-year-old Maine coon cat. Connie, Obie, and me: everything else was just background noise, especially Mom as she droned on and on about my fucking marks and why I didn't have any friends. I couldn't care less about school or friends. After what Mom and Dad called "Connie's incident," no one wanted to come to our house, anyway. After the shitstorm of Connie consorting with the devil, I could have had the decency to turn out semi-normal. I wanted to tell her that I was the one who had ended Connie's love affair — not with Satan, but an asshole dirt-biker from Beamsville.

While Mom droned on, I daydreamed about her and Dad getting old and dying and leaving the house to Connie and me so we could have the place all to ourselves. I even imagined myself hurrying things along, spooning stuff from the rat traps in the barn into the sugar Mom stirred into her tea and Dad sprinkled on oatmeal. Connie would cook the meals. I'd shop, tend the garden, and scare off trespassers who wanted to get a look at the infamous Connie Costello.

Three weeks ago, I got my wish. Not quite in the way I imagined, though. Dad died on the front lawn in the first onslaught, his mouth gaping in surprise as the swarm came in across that piss-yellow sky we now knew so well. Thinking it was an attack of locusts like in the Old Testament, he ran to the barn and dragged out foggers and pesticides, hoping to keep the swarm off the grapevines. But they weren't interested in anything that wasn't warm blooded. They went into his mouth and ears and straight down his throat. His body inflated like a balloon, then collapsed like a shucked corn husk. "Death by desiccation" was the phrase they used on the news.

When no one answered our 911 call or the messages we left with the pastor of Mom's church and the local funeral home, we buried Dad in the vineyard, where the ground was soft and easy to dig. Mom took to sitting in the front room watching TV and checking her iPad day and night with a Bible in her lap, while Connie and I boarded up the windows. They'd held up against the first onslaught, but the impact of so many tiny bodies had caused a web of fine cracks to appear. They sure wouldn't stand up to another attack.

From social media and TV, we found out that a second on-slaught was coming straight down at us from the north. It had already taken out Timmins, Sudbury, and North Bay, which hadn't had a chance to recover from the first onslaught before they were hit again. Outside of people who'd gone down mine shafts, the death toll was pretty much total. Car windshields shattered as if a million tiny rocks had hit them. Connie and I could see that pretty clearly whenever the trail came close to the road, which was jammed up with cars full of dried-out corpses. You might be able to drive off road in an armoured car or a tank, but a regular car, forget it. All cars did was give people a false sense of security. They thought that if they kept the win-dows rolled up, they'd be safe. Problem is, car windshields are made to crumble like sugar when they take a hit, not shatter like house windows. The first onslaught pretty much smashed through lines of cars as though the windows weren't even there, swarming passengers who were pinioned by exploding airbags.

We kept getting news for about a week, enough to know that the northeastern half of North America was covered by the onslaught. Something about the polar ice caps melting, releasing moth larvae that had been growing in there for millennia, maybe irradiated from nuclear waste from CANDU reactors they'd been burying in the Canadian Shield since the 1970s. That was one theory. Mom was certain it was God's judgment on humanity's evil, evil ways. I think maybe she was right, given what I've seen of so-called humanity over the last three weeks.

When TV and the internet disappeared, Mom started praying day and night. She told Connie and me that we had to go out and meet the swarm, that it was actually the way the Rapture was taking place and Dad was already up in Heaven at God's right hand, waiting for us; that he had spoken to her in a dream and urged us to join him in Paradise. Connie and I let her drag us outside when the sky went gold. When we saw the swarm on the horizon, we tried to pull Mom inside the house with us, but it was useless. She was engulfed like Dad, the moths forcing their way down her throat. She kept her hands clamped over her mouth but they found other places — ears, nostrils, eyes, up her skirt: anywhere they could reach her soft inner parts. Finally she opened her mouth to scream and in they went. Ate her up from the inside out. She fell to her knees like she was praying, pitched forward onto her face, and that was that. I finally had Connie and the house all to myself.

But like everyone else who didn't live in a windowless bunker, we either had to fortify our stronghold or start moving. Given that our store of food wasn't endless, and from what we'd heard before the news stopped coming — that the onslaught stopped somewhere south of Buffalo — we did what everyone else did: started riding our bikes on the recreational trail that followed the Welland Canal and Niagara River, eventually reaching the bridge over Niagara Falls. I took my passport, the Keep Calm mug, and Obie. With an onslaught happening every third or fourth day, we got good at reading the sky, knowing exactly how much time we had to take cover.

Nobody meant for the bike trail to become a highway, but once the real highways got blocked by cars, their gas tanks empty and drivers reduced to corn husks, what would you expect? Anyway, most of the other bikers were gone by the time we started out — either they had given up and left their bikes at the side of the trail, or got mowed down in an onslaught, or they were fast and fit enough to get south ahead of us.

Whatever. By week two, Connie and I were almost alone on the trail.

By then, we could calculate how much time we had to find a basement cantina or a shipping container or a public bathroom with a good solid door. Thick walls, no windows, preferably below ground level. Bathrooms were good because there was running water that was probably still clean. Connie said that wouldn't last long, with no one left working at the water filtration plants. She kept talking about stealing a water purifier from a sporting goods store. Yeah, right. Everyone had had exactly the same idea. In the Crappy Tires we managed to break in to, there was nothing left on the shelves but inflatable pool toys and Crock-Pots. Shit that no one needed anymore, if they ever had.

———————

Anyway, my punctured tire would have panicked me two weeks earlier, but I'd learned to keep calm and carry on. Which was why, when we heard the familiar roar of dirt bikes, I didn't immediately shit my pants. Connie's eyes widened and she jumped up, dropping the tube of glue. I picked it up and said, Stay calm, it's just dirt bikes.

What if someone recognizes me? asked Connie, her voice shaky.

I couldn't believe she could actually be more afraid of shaming by some stupid dirt-bikers than an onslaught.

They were on us in seconds. Two weasel-faced boys and a ratty-looking blond girl with her arms wrapped around one boy's waist. They roared past, then circled back. The boys looked about twenty, same as Connie. One had a bulky garbage bag strapped to his bike. The girl looked about fifteen — my age. She stared at me, mouth gaping.

Wassup, fellow refugees, said Boy One. Need help?

We're good, I answered, pumping my tire.

Boy Two nodded at my bulging pannier. Whatcha got there?

Candy, mostly. I shrugged.

Candy? The girl hopped off the bike.

Boy One grinned and said, Share and share alike.

The girl rummaged in my pannier.

Look at this! Oh Henry! Sugar. And what the fuck — Tampax! I just got my period.

Whoa, too much information, sis, said Boy Two.

Hungry? asked Boy One. We'll trade you some fresh meat for your sweet stuff.

Where'd you find meat? I asked.

Boy One grinned again. Hunted it down. Boom boom.

He tugged open the garbage bag. A black-and-tan leg fell out. Connie put her hands over her face. Ernst, she groaned.

Boy Two laughed. Oh, you know each other?

He had Ernst's collar looped around his handlebar.

You're a sick fuck, I said.

Get hungry enough, you'll eat anything. Even people, said Boy One.

Come with us to our buddy's house in Ridgeway, just off the trail, said Boy Two. Lotsa booze and a brick oven on the patio, where we'll roast Rover.

You know who we are? I asked.

Dessert? smirked Boy One.

Bay Two snickered.

My sister's Constanza Costello. I'm Mary Kate.

I crossed my arms and waited.

Holy shit, the Costello sisters, said Boy One.

Boy Two stared at Connie. You're that crazy chick who poisoned her boyfriend?

He had it coming, I said. Anyway, my sister was found innocent.

Everyone knows she's guilty, said Boy Two. And you think *we're* evil for killing a *dog*?

The boys jumped on their starters. As they roared off, their sister gave us the finger and tossed tampons behind her like a bride throwing a bouquet. I put them back in my now-empty pannier. They'd taken everything. Including the rat-sugar.

I looked up. The sky was the colour of an old bruise. We still had time.

Connie was crying. What do we do now?

Ride to Ridgeway. Find their buddy's house with the brick oven outside. Then, we wait.

For what? Connie asked.

For them to die, I told her.

UNLIMITED DREAM

Mark Sampson

The receptionist shoved her mass-market paperback under the desk as Ted approached, as if ashamed of the book's bright, trashy cover. There, inside the pod of her workstation, she tossed him a warm (if well-rehearsed) smile and confirmed that, yes, he was in the right place. Ted gave the girl his name and showed her some ID, and she made a few clicks into her computer before passing him a clipboard.

"Just fill this out and someone will be with you shortly," she said.

The clipboard, he noticed, held a printed form that he had already filled out twice at home, online.

This seemed to be the natural order of things now, he thought as he made himself comfortable in the waiting lounge — answering the same array of questions multiple times before interacting with one of these public–private initiatives. Ted's husband, Jeremy, said this likely had to do with corporate due diligence and legal liability, but Ted preferred to think it had more to do with him: with confirming and reconfirming that he was the right sort of person to participate in this initiative in the first place. As he poised the clipboard's tethered pen over the form, the questions before him felt like old friends now — predictable, unsurprising, almost soothing in the familiar cadence of their language:

- How many hours of sleep do you think you average per night?

  Less than 5 hours | 5 to 7 hours | More than 7 hours

- When you sleep, how often do you dream?

  Every night | 4 to 6 nights per week | 1 to 3 nights per week | Less than 1 night per week

- When you dream, do you usually have one dream per night, or several?

  One dream per night | Several dreams per night

- How would you rate the vividness of the majority of your dreams?

  Extremely vivid | Somewhat vivid | Not very vivid | Not vivid at all

- How likely are you to remember your dreams upon waking?

Very likely | Somewhat likely | Somewhat un-
likely | Not likely at all

On and on they went, more than three full pages, interrogating various aspects of Ted's nocturnal life. At the bottom of the final page, he found a comparatively unrelated question. It felt like a vestigial query from a bygone era, like some old chestnut endlessly repeated by a doddering, oblivious grandfather:

- In the last 14 days, have you experienced a fever, dry cough, or sudden loss of taste or smell?

Yes | No

Ted took the completed form back up to the receptionist, and she in turn put her embarrassing book down again, tucking it under some file folders.

There was no other way to describe the thing that the technician strapped to Ted's head: it looked like a large, stainless-steel colander. It had a wide, cone-shaped top that formed an inverted dome, its curved sides punctured by neat rows of tiny, circular holes. The base of the colander, the shape of a small suction cup, was also made of stainless steel and pinched Ted where it clasped him at the crown of his skull. The IV in his arm also pinched where the nurse had inserted it into the median cubital vein at Ted's elbow. The IV's thin, clear tube snaked up his shoulder before lifting off to the medical bag dangling from its

T-shaped stand at Ted's left. The bag, in turn, bulged with a strange, bright-pink solution.

"Are you comfortable?" the technician asked.

"Reasonably so," Ted replied.

The chair he was seated in looked — and leaned back — exactly like a dentist's chair. In fact, this little room could have passed for a dentist's workspace: small, sterile, with a computer screen featuring indecipherable software on a nearby desk, and multiple university degree certificates, written in impenetrable Latin, hanging on the wall above it. While Ted waited for the doctor, he rolled his eyes upward to try to get a glimpse of the colander again, which of course he couldn't. Fastened to his skull, the contraption was more a sensation now than a shape. But it did remind Ted of a joke that he and Jeremy sometimes made, a small idiolect that had arisen in their relationship over the years. It involved the popular phrase "cone of silence." Ted knew that neither he nor his husband could keep a secret to save their lives, and so whenever one of them had some juicy and potentially damaging gossip to share from their respective jobs or network of acquaintances, the other would quip, *Don't worry, bud, it's going into the colander of silence.* It always made them laugh, this idea of secrets pouring out of them as if through holes in a strainer. Of course, the colander strapped to Ted was not designed to let something *out*, but rather to bring something *in*.

The physician entered the room then, accompanied by the nurse who had set up Ted's IV. "Mr. McMichael, I'm Dr. Tadros," he said brusquely as he seated himself onto a small, padded stool, then wheeled over. "Are you comfortable?"

"Reasonably so," Ted repeated.

"Excellent. Then let us begin." Dr. Tadros looked up and nodded sternly at the nurse and the technician.

The latter reached over to a small electronic device attached to the side of the medical bag and keyed in some numbers.

When she did, Tadros glared at her. "*Excuse* me, not the two-oh-two — the one-forty-seven, please," he barked, his voice laced with impatience.

"Sorry, Doctor." She made the adjustment.

The neon-pink fluid in the medical bag flowed through the tube and into Ted's arm. As it did, he felt almost immediately drowsy, his eyelids growing heavy as if sodden with rain. Dr. Tadros leered in close to examine his patient's quickly dilating pupils. At this proximity, Ted could see that the physician was somewhere in his mid-seventies, a fact he was trying to hide via an extraordinarily bad dye job that he had perpetrated against his hair, goatee, and even his eyebrows. He also had ancient acne scars that pocked his cheeks, as well as the breath of a man who thought Tic Tacs caused impotence. Whether it was the phony hair colour, the halitosis, or the harsh way Tadros had spoken to his staff, Ted decided to dislike the doctor. *How vain do you have to be,* he wondered as he nodded off, *to dye your eyebrows?*

But soon he was asleep, and the unlimited dream began. It was exactly as the officials with the public–private initiative had told Ted it would be, only more so. The phantasm that rushed into his mind was soft and warm and welcoming, yet angular, full of dimension, as intense as any dream he'd ever had. In it, he was a child again, only this wasn't quite his childhood. He wasn't quite himself. Here, he was somehow … *better*, a kinder version of who he actually was, and so were his parents. He noticed it immediately, how accepting of and compassionate they were toward Ted, and each other. It was so *strange*. Also, their house was their house, only it wasn't. It was bigger, cleaner, better appointed. Among its furnishings was a lengthy dining-room table, and in the dream this table was loaded with food they'd never seemed to have when Ted was a kid — a huge, elaborate meal for Christmas or Thanksgiving. Steaming slices of turkey fresh off the bird, sweet potatoes, boiled beans, fresh salad, and cornbread stuffing: it all lay before him on great platters or in ornate bowls. Young Ted, starved for that bounty, loaded up a plate, sat down, and gorged himself. His parents encouraged it, their voices brimming with love and gratitude — emotions in short supply during his real child-hood. He wanted to linger here, to bask in this vivid place. But then the dream shifted and he was outside, in the sun, running through some sort of field, huge and verdant — maybe a vineyard in Bordeaux or an orchard in the Annapolis Valley. He moved gleefully through rows of plants and trees. He saw berries on the vine, fruit on the branch, lush and ripe and ready to fall into the world's waiting hands. He stopped, reached up, and plucked off its stem something that he couldn't see. Raising whatever it was to his mouth, Ted bit down. He could practically feel the juice disgorge down his chin, warm and sticky and sweet.

Then he awoke. Only a few seconds had passed since he'd gone under. Ted felt the technician's hands on his shoulders to lean him forward in the chair so that Tadros could reach inside the colander. He rooted around in there; Ted sensed the doctor's impatient grasping along the sides of the stainless steel. For a moment, Tadros looked panicked that he'd find the colander empty, but then his hand landed on something and he pulled it out.

It was a piece of fruit, an enormous and shapely Bartlett pear. Even with his eyes half-open, Ted could see the pear was greener than any green should naturally be, and it had no stem.

He would have kept his eyes on this queer object had it not been for the pain he suddenly noticed somewhere below him. He looked down and saw that the nail on his left index finger was bleeding, and the nurse had just moved in to cover it with a Band-Aid. *Was I chewing on my finger in my sleep?* Ted wondered. *I was, wasn't I?*

"Extraordinary," Dr. Tadros said as he examined the pear in the fluorescent light above their heads. "A perfect piece of fruit, and perfectly edible."

At this, Tadros took a greedy bite of the pear, then offered it to the nurse and the technician, and they did the same, each stealing a single munch over Ted's prone body before returning the pear to the doctor.

"Let's book him in for his second appointment," Tadros said, smacking his lips. "Mr. McMichael, how do you feel?"

"I'm hungry too," he replied.

But Tadros flinched back as if electrocuted, clutching the pear to his chest like a child holding a treat he wasn't willing to share.

Despite the now regular injuries to Ted's fingers, Jeremy was miffed that he himself was ineligible to participate in the unlimited dream. "It's not fair," he said one night at dinner.

"I know," Ted said. "I hear you. But the rules are the rules."

It wasn't that Ted's husband had scored poorly on what was now officially called the Tadros Dream Vividness Scale. Jeremy had gotten a respectable 8.7 on the TDVS, enough to generate half a supermarket's worth of meat, fruit, and veg in a single eight-hour sitting. Rather, he'd been disqualified because of his poor sleep patterns, the circadian rhythms messed up by a job he couldn't afford to quit. After getting laid off two years earlier at the architectural firm where he'd been since graduating university, Jeremy was forced to take work as a security guard in a condo tower, where he rotated through three unforgiving seven-day shifts (eight to four, four to midnight, midnight to eight) before getting seven days off. This, naturally, had wreaked havoc with his sleep.

"I don't understand why someone doesn't just pay me not to work, so I can help feed the world," he said, and not for the first time.

"Hey, you're preaching to the choir," Ted replied, sipping his wine. Unfortunately, after the most recent pandemic, governments and private enterprises had long developed an aversion to paying people not to work.

Yet, the world *needed* to be fed. Following the Fourth Great Drought and the Third Great Flood, most of Africa, India, and Eastern Europe were in dire straits. The public–private initiative had developed the unlimited dream to ameliorate the situation and were seeing some great results. Approximately 485,000 people across the US and Canada had both the minimum TDVS score of 7.5 and the proper sleep patterns to qualify for the unlimited dream, and most had stepped up to do their duty. In one eight-hour session, that many people could generate enough food to feed Africa, India, and Eastern Europe for a month or more.

But there was a catch, one that preyed on both Ted's and Jeremy's minds: those who dreamed up "conjured food," as it was now called, were not allowed to eat conjured food. Something truly horrible would happen if they did, though officials were tight-lipped about exactly what. This was not a problem as long as the food was shipped overseas to deal with famines on the other side of the world. But should those famines strike North America, as the climate scientists assured everyone they would, and conjured food became the only food available, people like Ted would have nothing to eat at all.

"See, that's another reason it's good you're not participating," he told Jeremy. "If conjured food takes over our supermarkets, I'll have to starve. I'll just whittle away to nothing. Do you want that happening to you?"

"Don't make jokes," Jeremy grumbled back.

But it was no joke. The near half-million North Americans participating in the unlimited dream knew what they had signed up for. But it was a small sacrifice as far as Ted was concerned. Officially, he was being brave and selfless and doing his duty. Unofficially, he was doing it for the dreams themselves. This was a secret that had gone into the cone rather than the colander of silence inside his mind — he hadn't even shared it with his own husband. Thanks to Ted's staggering 27.7 TDVS score, his visions during the unlimited dream had hooked him like heroin. The food, the drink, the passions and paracosms, the alternate reality that eddied through his head during those eight-hour sessions were nothing short of a bacchanal. In those dreams, Ted was leading a different life. He was happier, more fulfilled, and with memories of the past he could actually treasure. In the dreams, he still spoke to his parents on a regular basis. He had childhood friends. In the dreams, he often had a more rewarding and remunerative job. He was also married to somebody else. This should have unsettled Ted, only it didn't. His "dream husband" was more confident, more successful and, yes, more attractive than Jeremy. Ted *hated* leaving that man at the end of a session.

Indeed, awakening from an unlimited dream was like a kind of mourning for Ted, an almost molecular disappointment that he had left these phantasms behind and returned to the bland, austere reality of his actual life. How could you share something like that with your spouse?

As for the post-session injuries? They were, as far as Ted was concerned, just another sacrifice. The straps to the chairs that Dr. Tadros's team had introduced were certainly cutting down on participants' self-inflicted wounds, and Ted looked forward to a time when his fingers weren't constantly wrapped in bandages. But even if that time never came, Ted wouldn't mind. He thought there was something almost poetic about it all — how helping the helpless, the less fortunate, the starving masses on the other side of the world would engender a desire for ... well, there was no other term for it. A desire for self-cannibalism.

———————

By Ted's seventeenth session, so many people were participating in the unlimited dream that they had to move group sessions to an abandoned hangar, filthy and poorly lit, out near the airport. Rows upon rows of people reclined in their dentists' chairs all along the hangar floor, colanders strapped to their heads. From a distance, that floor might have resembled an endless field of small satellite dishes pointing toward the heavens — except for the pneumatic tubes placed inside each colander, to pump out food that arrived from the unlimited dream and into large bins and movable freezers lining the perimeter of the hangar. Lab coat–sporting scientists roamed the floor with their clipboards and tablets, and Dr. Tadros himself watched the proceedings from a catwalk above their heads. Above *him*, tarps were tied down over the hangar's dilapidated metal roof, to keep the rain out.

Ted knew something was amiss when he was wrenched out of his dream less than an hour in, by the sound of someone screaming. He tilted his head up and forced his eyes open, despite the dream's almost unholy power to suck him back down into its pleasures. When he did, he saw two lab coats race past him and down the aisle with expressions of concern on their faces. Looking around, Ted saw that most other participants were still asleep, though a few had also stirred awake to the sound of the commotion. As his eyes tried to focus, Ted could see down the aisle that someone, a man in his mid-fifties, had broken free of his straps and was climbing out of his chair. The scientists were trying to restrain his arms, but the man proved surprisingly strong despite his lithe, wiry frame. Ted watched as he shoved a scientist to the floor and then raised one of his arms to his mouth. It was almost comical until it wasn't: how he bit into his own wrist, then, like a cartoon vampire. Blood leaped and splattered over his face, the liquid almost black in the hangar's grim light. By then, Dr. Tadros had rushed down the catwalk and was tearing across the floor, bellowing instructions as he did.

Something must have shifted in the IV fluid pumping into Ted's body, because he grew groggy once again. Just before the unlimited dream swallowed him up and saturated him with another delightful fantasy, he saw the now-bleeding man race over to the bins and grab the first vegetable he could, a great frond of kale. He was just lifting the leafy green to his bloodstained mouth when another clutch of scientists tackled him to the floor.

"They called it a *what*?" Jeremy asked at breakfast the next morning.

"A hallucination."

"Seriously?"

"Well, not a hallucination. That's not the word they used. They called it a 'meta-dream.' They said that I was dreaming *inside* my dream — that my dream-self was having a nightmare." At this, Jeremy looked incredulous, but Ted pressed on. "They claimed there *was* no man biting into his own wrist or trying to steal a piece of kale. They said I 'imagined' the whole thing."

"Really?"

"Yep." Ted paused and cleared his throat. "Except ..."

"Except?"

Ted stared into his mug of tea, which Jeremy had brewed for him. Jeremy had brewed the tea and made the breakfast (Eggos and microwaved bacon, but still) despite looking ready for bed himself, having just finished the dreaded midnight-to-eight shift at the condo building.

"Except?" he asked again.

"Except ... when we were in line to get back on the bus, I chatted up a couple of people who'd been seated near me during the unlimited dream. Jeremy, they'd woken up too. They ... they said they saw the *exact* same thing I did. But how could that be? How could three people all have the same 'meta-dream,' the same nightmare at the same time?" He looked up into his husband's face. "I think Dr. Tadros's 'meta-dream' theory is as phony as his hair colour."

"Teddy, you need to quit. I know we like the extra money, but this isn't right. We'll figure something else out. You can't do this anymore."

That made a lot of sense. Ted suspected that the "meta-dream" wasn't the only thing Dr. Tadros and the public–private initiative were lying about. For Ted, for *everyone*, the bigger mystery was what would happen if a participant in the unlimited dream actually ate a piece of conjured food. Rumours ran the gamut from sickness and death for the individual to an "extinction-level" event for everyone on Earth. *One bite could kill us all* was the most extreme conjecture, and the powers that be did nothing to dissuade it.

But Ted would not quit, and he could not bear to tell Jeremy the real reason why. He could not bring himself to admit that the life inside the unlimited dream was so much better than their own. During his waking hours, Ted found that he thought about his *other* husband, the spouse who lived inside his head, *all the time*. Longing for him, yearning to spend those lengthy hours together felt … felt, well, like a *hunger*.

"I'm helping to feed the world," he told Jeremy instead. "J, billions of people are relying on us. We can't stop now."

At this, Jeremy could only shake his head.

Ted started by telling them he was cold, which wasn't a lie. The hangar did get drafty, especially now that autumn had come on. In response, they gave him a simple black blanket, thin, insubstantial, like the kind in plastic baggies handed out on an airplane. It would do. Ted removed the blanket from the bag and smoothed its cheap fabric over his torso and limbs, making sure to hide where the IV connected to his left arm.

Several minutes later, he told another technician who popped by that he wasn't quite ready to go under.

"Do you want me to do your straps in the meantime?" the technician asked, and Ted shuffled a shoulder over the hem of the blanket to show one part of a strap, to say that, nope, someone had already come by earlier to do them. This *was* a lie, but the technician bought it. She seemed harried, impatient, eager to get on to the next person in the next chair. There were more than a thousand participants in the hangar that day, and the public–private initiative was short-staffed.

Finally, with his right hand, Ted reached across his belly, now hidden by the blanket. With his thumb and index finger, he pinched shut the IV tube leading into his left arm. But then he freaked out a little. He let go of the tube for a moment before seizing it again in his pincer-like grip. Could he really go through with this? Could he turn down what awaited him inside the hedonistic delirium of the unlimited dream? Ted let go of the tube yet again as more doubt washed over him.

Another scientist, on the outskirts of Ted's peripheral vision, loomed suddenly into view. She flipped a switch on the machine attached to Ted's IV bag, and the neon-pink solution raced into the tube. Ted scrambled his arm back across his belly and seized the plastic once again to cut off the flow, but a trace amount of the otherworldly liquid managed to get through. He had never participated in the unlimited dream with such a small quantity of the fluid in his system. Had anyone? He felt his panic come back once more, filling his mouth with a coppery terror.

It was the hunger alone — not the drowsiness, and certainly not the warm, velvety paracosm that would envelop him immediately after — that set in. Ted felt the starvation amp through his body like electricity, and within a few seconds he was struggling to stay in his chair. He cursed the undone straps then. What had he been *thinking*?

Just relax, a voice in his head spoke up. It was Jeremy's, offering some of his earnest spousal wisdom. *If you're going to do this, then do it. Stay awake. Look around. See what they're really up to. The hunger isn't real, bud. You don't know real hunger. You're awake, so observe your surroundings. That's what you promised yourself you'd do.*

So Ted did just that. He turned his head from side to side, the colander moving with him, and looked at the now-drowsing people, his neighbours in the rows of reclining chairs on either side of him. They were, every last one, struggling against the straps. Perhaps inside their heads, they were delighting in the reverie of the unlimited dream, but from the outside they looked as though they were ready to kill or maim, to tear free of their chairs and begin cannibalizing themselves or each other.

The machine at Ted's IV bag began to beep maniacally. He looked down and saw that the plastic tube, above where it met the blanket, had bulged like a goitre under the weight of the pink solution now trapped there. It looked like it might burst. Panic flared through Ted again and he released the tube. The liquid rushed into him all at once, and he expected it to knock him out and send him careening into the unlimited dream. But it didn't. It simply caused his hunger to roar up louder than before.

A technician jogged over to see what all the beeping was about, but she froze at the sound of something else. Three rows over from Ted, a large woman had torn herself out of her chair, the noise of ripping Velcro and her screams filling the air of the hangar. The technician rushed over to help the others who were now trying to pin the woman back down.

Ted knew this was his moment. They were distracted. They didn't see him cast off his blanket and scramble out of his seat.

About twenty feet away, somebody was pushing a bin on wheels toward the side doors of the hangar. The bin was already full, stacked high with a pile of large, ripe mangos. Their skins were a bright, ruby red.

Ted broke into a sprint toward the bin. Someone behind him bellowed. *Hey. Hey! Stop him! Somebody stop that man!*

The person pushing the bin halted and looked up. He had no time to react as Ted raced over. Ted leaped into the air, pivoted, and then bodychecked the man like one hockey player slamming into another. The man pinwheeled around and crashed knees first onto the floor before hitting his face on the concrete.

Ted barely noticed, and felt no sympathy for the man anyway. He was too busy reaching into the bin and fetching out the nearest mango he could find.

He raised the fruit to his mouth, not worrying about the skin that lay between him and the luscious orange flesh beneath. He bared his teeth.

But then Dr. Tadros himself appeared before him, having rushed down the catwalk. The good doctor — now a kind of quasi-celebrity, beloved and loathed by the unwashed masses in equal measure — looked even older and frailer than Ted remembered. He certainly looked too old and frail to wrestle Ted to the floor. *Wow*, he thought, *that really is a bad dye job. Who does he think he's fooling?*

"*No!*" the physician yelled, raising both hands as if he were being robbed. "That's not yours! That's not for you to eat! *That's not for you!*"

But it was too late. Ted sank his teeth into the mango, seizing it like a dog with a bone. He ripped the skin back and nestled his teeth into the fruit's flesh. The sticky juice erupted into his mouth and spattered his chin. His roiling hunger welcomed that first morsel as he gnashed it into a pulp and then forced it down his esophagus.

Ted looked up suddenly, his eyes widening. In one single moment, the entire hangar had gone white, as if consumed by a nuclear flash. It was like a great fire had come out of nowhere and eaten the entire world.

No, that wasn't right. It wasn't a fire. It was a great, glowing tunnel, a swirling, ethereal corridor that had begun radiating out of a nearby wall and presenting itself to Ted like a flower. He looked into it and somehow knew, knew *instantly*, what awaited him at the other end of that churning passageway. He knew *who* awaited him there.

He thought of Jeremy, but only for a second or two. Poor Jeremy. He'd take this hard.

But then Ted began to walk toward the tunnel, toward the eye of his new life, the mango still in his hand. He bowed his head and took another bite.

MARIANNE IS NOT HUNGRY

Jowita Bydlowska

1

I don't need to talk about all the boring details about who I am and why I am; no one is asking Air to explain itself. But I will talk about who I am in relation to Marianne because Marianne treats me differently from most people. And I treat her differently too.

When Marianne tries to be optimistic about me, she says I am Energy or Fuel.

I like being referred to as Energy or Fuel. In that incarnation, Marianne likes to dream of me as little tight packets of zaps, hisses, and sparkles from a broken electrical wire all jammed together. Or she pictures pellets of oil, like laundry pods. As packets of energy or pellets of fuel, I wouldn't spill, stain, cause indigestion, aversion, allergy; I wouldn't choke anybody. I'd be fully utilitarian and all Marianne would have to do is open a small cupboard where she'd keep me in sleek, silky boxes similar to Apple-computer packaging. Inside, I'd be lined up in neat rows, the variation of shapes not exceeding five — a diamond, a heart, an oval, a square, a rectangle — and all of us would be the same weight of ten grams, same caloric output of … Marianne hasn't decided yet of what; this is the part that has always been problematic.

But I am not in a rush. I am impossible to get rid of. Marianne has tried to fight me many times but in the end she always eats and eats eats eats eats. Last time she went a week without me, she relapsed on a tulle dress of wettish lettuce leaves, sewn with white membrane and vaginal-pink endocarp of grapefruit. A prom for one! Marianne drank two litres of Coke Zero and danced with conviction like you do at a prom, danced hard like you do in a fat camp. Later, Marianne did the calorie math and it was in the range of three hundred, which was three hundred more than she needed to no longer fear me.

But am I the enemy? Not quite. The enemy is the absence of me, what shows up when I'm not around, a wound the size of Marianne's heart. What says: I'm not enough and always too much. Unjustly, Marianne has said in therapy that it is me who controls her. Everyone else just eats me. Enjoys me, perverts me.

But it's Marianne who perverts me. And it's Hunger that controls her, eats her.

2

Marianne is on an internet date with a cool cryptocurrency type who is ten years her junior. The restaurant is called

Hello123, which strikes Marianne as uninspired, like calling a place Abcdwhatever.

As for me, here I am all bowls of grain and various sprouts. Her eyes magnify, double and triple me when I enter her mouth; she wishes for grain and seeds to expand in her belly, fill her up to stave away the need for me.

Marianne orders a smoothie that has seven ingredients, three of them unpronounceable. The dishes are named after healthy things that are supposed to happen to the eaters, such as Detox, Relax, Happy. Marianne's smoothie is Happy. She is doubtful it will work.

Her date has long hair and a neck tattoo, and he is pretty in a dopey way, big brown eyes. His nose is red at the tip, and wet. He reminds Marianne of a doe.

Marianne talks about going to the new modern art museum located in a former chocolate factory behind the restaurant, where you can pay twenty dollars to see videos of people screaming silently at wool, or stare at pebbles arranged in piles and patterns in severe rooms with metal lockers lining the walls.

Yeah, I guess we could go, her date says as if they've known each other for twelve years and she is exhausting him. His name is Eric, which Marianne first heard as "Derrick." Marianne wonders what his penis looks like.

3

On another date, Marianne eats ice cream. Only one scoop. She tells her date she doesn't have much of a sweet tooth. For a while, she can think only of the ice cream, so I am more important than the guy, another internet find — this one a film type with scraggly hair.

Marianne tells the guy about her fuel pods idea: This would be a ritual, like prayer, taking out one of those pods. I would have to dress up, put makeup on, do my hair. I would wear high heels. There would be a clean tablecloth every time. I would have a porcelain plate with gold-leaf trimming. Or should I go more contemporary; should I have a black, modern plate, utensils made out of concrete to only signal the idea of eating? Food pods. You would save so much time.

No, this is not about time. I want eating to be an aesthetic experience, but like visiting a museum, not a restaurant, Marianne says and in the same moment worries the guy will think she feels the same way about sex. Then she remembers I placate most people. She suggests a snack. She hopes that suggesting ice cream and then a snack will strike the guy as eccentric, a little wild; here's a girl who doesn't care for rules.

Marianne is good at banter, and she knows when to say disarming, self-deprecating things that, for a special Marianne flavour, she likes to mix with vulgarisms.

For example, she says, I probably have daddy issues. It's because my daddy left when I was five. Who could blame him? I used to spy on him in the bathroom, was obsessed with trying to catch a glimpse of his penis.

Marianne knows that the guy is now probably thinking about Marianne as a little girl; Marianne's daddy — there is a daddy and he can fuck you up; Marianne looking at penises; and then he's thinking about his own penis. He is thinking about Marianne touching his penis. Then Marianne's daddy, again.

The guy says, T.M.I. much? He says it like that, in the abbreviation, and both he and Marianne laugh at how terrible that sounds, both of them trying to skate over the awkwardness of Marianne's statement and his discomfort.

The guy moves his body closer as they walk; Marianne notices even the subtlest vibrations in the atmosphere.

Marianne's looks are not problematic even when she throws up for prolonged periods of time. Throwing up too much causes swelling of the parotid glands, which often gives Marianne's slightly gaunt face a fuller look, like she's got silicone fillers.

She is tall for a woman, she dresses in slim skirts and slim jackets, she has slim feet.

She wears ugly eyeglasses. This is also for a perverse reason: only someone who wants to make it appear she doesn't care about looks would wear such ugly eyeglasses. Only someone approachable. This is good news for the guy; this is good news for all the guys.

This guy has a car, a VW SUV, which is exactly the kind of car Marianne thought he would have. Only a little edgy, safe, expensive but not too expensive.

She thinks of the guy as "Steve," which is not a name that inspires sex; his real name is a better name: Felix.

They drive to a place called the Hole in the Wall and they order charcuterie and Marianne calculates it'll be approximately four hundred calories each, plus the three-fifty for the ice cream. Steve-Felix talks about a short film he's making, something about a frog stealing diamonds; it's a parabolic tale; the diamonds are desire, there are Catholic dogma themes in it. In her head, Marianne gives Felix a makeover, trims his beard, which reminds her of straight pubic hair she's seen in some Japanese porn.

Felix drives Marianne to her apartment and she asks if she can kiss him. She always kisses men she goes on dates with; her tongue, a receipt for the date being printed out.

4

Marianne sends a *more-as-a-friend* text to Felix. He instantly agrees to be relegated. He says he just wants to be around. Then he is around all the time — art galleries, park walks, bookstores, B-movies — and then he takes pictures of her face, and then they are in his bed, where he goes down on Marianne and doesn't make her come. But that night, for the first time since university, Marianne is reckless with me. At 2:00 a.m., they drive to an all-night diner and order crepes that come out of the kitchen two minutes later. They both wonder why it's taken such a short amount of time to prepare me. Were the crepes just ready, sitting under heat bulbs? The crepes taste fine. Marianne and Felix come home and fuck and it is good. Again Marianne doesn't come but she is very close.

5

Marianne neglects me when she is in love. Also, she can spend hours looking at pornography, trying to find the right image or video clip — as with me, Marianne prefers a variety of flavours of flesh. When she is preoccupied with the matters of heart or sex, she feels light-headed, and when she thinks of me, she feels full. And grateful she doesn't need me.

But I am patient. I know that Marianne's happy states don't last forever, and that there will be time when Marianne, again, will spend most of her time with me, thinking of me; when she will count calories instead of wondering how to tell Felix how to trim his beard without hurting his feelings, which is what she's thinking about right now, her belly filled with tonkotsu ramen, at a thousand calories.

Felix doesn't know that Marianne hasn't eaten anything prior to their date, and that tonkotsu sinks into her the way fresh rain sinks into porous concrete — this is something Marianne has an image of whenever she eats MSG-bombed foods that fill then instantly feel empty. She grew up in a place with lots of concrete around; she watched many rainfalls from the inside of a drainage ring at a construction site by her apartment building, where she'd sit eating bags of sawdust-like yellow potato chips, the first food she ever binged on.

After tonkotsu, Marianne and Felix go back to Felix's place where Marianne gives him a blow job — one tablespoon of semen, twenty-five calories. When they cuddle afterward, Felix tries to pinch Marianne's non-stomach and makes a joke about throwing up. He accuses Marianne of eating and not gaining weight. Marianne feels grateful again.

6

Marianne is starting to really like Felix and she is scared of that. She makes plans to see the young guy, Eric. At Eric's place, you clap your hands and a wall lights up in a neon design that looks like a formula of a chemical equation. He says it's called Nanoleaf.

He puts on a movie. They sit side by side on a couch. He pulls out his phone and starts texting. His pit bull slobbers over and sits beside Marianne, all teeth and a felt face. The pit bull is named after a pastry.

The movie is about alien plants. There is a famous actress in it whose nose turns pink when she cries and when that happens, she looks eerily similar to Eric. In the movie, the actress's bearded husband is eaten by a flower.

Eric places a hand on Marianne's breast. Instantly, she turns to face him, as if he'd pressed a button. They kiss, and his dog makes a noise that sounds approving. Marianne wants to ask the guy to put his dog in a cage or in her own bedroom — she's not sure where the dog lives but she probably has her own bedroom.

Later on, upstairs in Eric's bedroom, he undresses, folds his clothes. Marianne wonders if he is a sociopath. He isn't her first sociopath. She doesn't come, and she doesn't feel like she is even close, the way she's felt with Felix. Before leaving, she takes a picture of the dog and then of the neon lights.

On the way home, she decides to go back to Hello123 for a night smoothie. While she waits for the one called Calm, she looks at the walls, all wood panelling, which makes her think *skinned trees*. There's wetness between her legs, Eric dripping out of her.

I arrive. Marianne sucks on the straw and thinks of Felix and of lying down next to him and tugging on his cheerful, stubby penis, and him gently guiding her head toward it, asking her the whole time if this is okay — Eric didn't ask once. Marianne wrinkles her nose.

7

If you only knew, Felix! Marianne lets me overtake her only once since she met you. She isn't even hungry — imagine that!

Listen, before you, she never experienced such discipline. Never! I'm sure it's related to the fact that before you, she's never truly orgasmed in that deep, spiritual — her words — way she has with you. Because that's what happened, Felix, and you don't even know it, you think she's been climaxing all this time and the way she grabbed your head and sobbed into your shoulder, you just chalked it up to a particularly strong one when, in fact, it was her first one with you and the first one like that ever. She felt it in her core, she had thoughts that embarrassed her, the word "soul" came up. Felix — Felix, she has never thought about me less since you showed up! Yes, she has grouped all your dates according to my various appearances — Cuban sandwiches, ramen, Japanese grill, ramen, scallops, beet soup, sushi, momos, curry, ramen, ramen, ramen — but I was secondary to her falling in love.

But we are here to talk about the slip. On the evening I manage to slime into her, in my Jabba the Hutt Hunger — my open and bottomless throat, my familiarity with Marianne's parameters of sanity — you are away.

Marianne starts with a salad, too much lettuce, followed up by three grapefruits. These are permitted. She feels full, which is not a feeling she likes. An intense debate in Marianne's head: to let me stay or to pile more of me on top of what's there, to the point that she'll have to empty the contents. If she decides to pile up, that means I'll be sending out bad boys, swagger boys walking into the saloon with our trans-fat slingshot guns, our caloric cowboy hats, our sugar whores, our creams and sauces.

And off she goes — she is opening the fridge and pulling out packaged ravioli, and she feels dizzy, giddy and rebellious and ashamed at the same time. Felix, if only you could see her! She is doing what you've accused her of doing, what she hasn't done ever since she fell in love with you.

First, Marianne fills a bowl with baby carrots, also known as "orange markers" (Cheetos are also "orange markers" and so are oranges), which is food that once it shows up, lets her know when it's safe to stop purging. She eats the carrots fast, so fast that she gets hiccups. The base is set. She waits ten minutes. After the waiting is over, it's finally time for the rest, where anything goes as long as it fills an unfillable essence.

There isn't a lot of intricate planning to Marianne's binges, but there's a little bit of it. The bad-boy foods are usually soft, like stomachs that grow from eating too many of them. Carbohydrates, croissants, cheeses. Often, there is one special thing, something slightly unusual and also forbidden. Today it's something called pizzelle — light, sugary wafers engraved with pretty designs of flowers — which she will eat with ravioli, and marshmallows and cashews. The cashews are the worst to purge, which is why Marianne packages them between the ravioli and marshmallows, the two things that will hopefully take the shard-y nuts with them for the ride out of Marianne's throat.

How does Marianne consume me? She's compared it to a blackout, no thought and no real pleasure, yet complete abandon. She tastes but subtlety is lost; this is not about appreciation.

After she's done consuming, Marianne checks her phone and when a text from you comes through, she gets cramps, and then guilt floods her body, gets into her fingertips. She runs to the bathroom and purges. A nail scraping the back of her throat, her stomach muscles contracting. She looks in the mirror to check on her face, which swells and turns darker and darker, her mascara running, the whites of her eyes pink and smaller.

The strange thing, she didn't even feel the hunger — something in her body drove her to it but it's two weeks before her period, so it's not that. As usual, she wonders if it's possible to choke on me and die, and what would she look like, swollen and stiff in a puddle. What she worries about the most is breaking her face; it's an indignity she thinks is unnecessary.

8

It's been years since she's eaten without any guilt, although she still remembers that time — how blissful it was to not care. She lived with Lucien then and they made midnight grilled-cheese sandwiches and she could eat two or three, and the rest of the time they spent in her single bed, exploring each other's bodies. She didn't love Lucien but the sex was nice. Lucien used to say she could wear a garbage bag over — her face? her body? She wasn't sure — and she would still be the most beautiful girl in the world. Marianne thought that compliment extreme; she didn't want to be dressed in black plastic, she wanted to show off her body, except eventually she didn't because the midnight grilled-cheese sandwiches started to catch up with her and the body became larger and softer, her thighs were cliché thunderous and she grew breasts. During that time, Marianne went to a bar and was offered a job waitressing because of her cleavage. Up until then, she had never experienced the power of having breasts — it seemed absurd to her that gaining an inch of fat and two new globes of flesh could mean a significant financial improvement, but it did. The waitressing tips were excellent.

9

Right now, Marianne is feeling faint but her fingertips are filled with electricity escaping her body. She needs to lie down. The cashews have scratched her throat badly. It's a good thing you are not telepathic, Felix — can't see into space and time.

In your text you tell her you got her a really lovely gift in Miami, where you are working on a documentary about dancers in small towns of America.

Unlike Marianne's previous boyfriends, you travel for work and she thinks she will like that because she enjoys longing; it is predictability and having to constantly share space with a man that causes her to relapse into me. With a man always around, Marianne needs to hide, needs to have her secrets because she lets men swallow her whole; she is to them what I am to her, she is their food. She likes being their food but even food needs rest; I need a rest from Marianne although I am already reminding her that she will need to take care of her emptiness, her stomach catching on quickly that it has been deprived of me. Her stomach is angry for having been cheated by the feeling of satiety and the hormones released from her digestive tract that have signalled she is full. She's Schrödinger's cat of deprivation — having just eaten but not having eaten at all. Her stomach staggers into the saloon of need, swinging; it kicks the door open with an angry boot of hunger.

She texts back that she's about to watch TV and she dutifully turns on Netflix and finds a show about people in a bake-off competition. She watches and eats with her eyes, her ears; she repeats the words "buttercream" and "caramelized" in her head. One of the chefs makes a cake in the shape of a pie, complete with edible tinfoil; another chef makes pastries that look like bacon and eggs; there is also a cake that pretends to be an albino boa constrictor.

10

After that one slip, Marianne doesn't binge and purge for a long time. She wants her new relationship to be different, pure, and she wants to be in her body. When you come back, Felix, she waits for you in your bed, half-naked. She is proud of her restraint. She has bought barbari bread, moose jerky, things in little containers, a Persian spinach dip called borani esfenaj, eesti kartulisalat, an Estonian potato salad ... I have to be perverse and special, me, which she doesn't eat, which makes her look sophisticated, interesting.

You fuck her and she is so happy to have you inside her — so happy she is unable to sleep most of the night.

This situation repeats itself, the fucking and Marianne's euphoric sleeplessness, the weird dishes piling up in your fridge. The weird dishes are getting wetter, softer, smellier, as neither of you eats much. Marianne suspects that you also do weird stuff with me, or that something I do to you makes you pull the sheets over your legs, or how you hate it when she touches your stomach, when she especially marvels over the soft hole in the left side where you had your appendix taken out. You smack her hand away gently when she presses her finger into it. Fucking stop it, you hiss. She doesn't do it again but she looks at the sweet little dip every time she sucks your cock; it makes her suck harder, with more dedication; she feels sad over the scar, she wants to compensate for it by giving you the nicest blow job ever.

You tell her you love her and she tells you she loves you and you send each other pictures of rescue dogs you'd like to adopt. You even try to write her a little poem on the back of a postcard of *My Room at the Beau-Rivage* by Matisse.

Nothing is ordinary
Not even the sun, the November chill, the river,
The constellation of your freckles
This poem is stupid. I can't write poems.

Everything you do together is a celebration, the way everything is with a new couple: waking up, dressing, a bath; going out to a coffee shop to read books side by side is a celebration, a visit to IKEA is a celebration, a visit to a mall can be an art performance.

On the way home from the mall, you make a detour and get an order of onion rings from a drive-through and you have your first fight.

It's junk food, she says darkly.

It's just onion rings.

It's death.

That night, you tell her that her insomnia is exhausting, her tossing and turning. You don't sleep, you don't eat, how do you survive? you say to her — you don't yell.

On love alone, Marianne says, and this must be true. Marianne notices your snarl and from now on, she will always notice it.

11

The second time Felix is away, Marianne doesn't eat much. After all, she survives on love alone. She buys a dress fit for a ballerina, with a short skirt, a wrap top that shows off her ribs, the lack of breasts. She sends the picture to Felix.

Jesus!

?

Felix is shooting B-roll, fill-in footage for the film about the dancers in small towns of America, aerial shots of roads and forests and mountains, panning of the camera over the chaos of unwashed dishes in various trailer-park sinks, broken plastic toys in yards with balding yellow patches of grass, tutus draped over broken chairs, close-ups of signs, close-up hands on the wheel, a diner and in it booths, a red-and-blue jukebox, its swoosh of selection cards, "Stand by Your Man," fingers dropping sugar cubes into coffees. And endless girl legs, skinny, thick, and bowed: pliés, relevés, sautés.

> Just kidding. Cute dress. One more I love
> you: I love you!

I love you! she texts back, balls up the ballerina dress. She opens the kitchen cupboards, marvels at my absence.

She goes to the organic store around the corner. She grabs a box and shops like one of the women she always sees walking in and out of the store, their canvas bags filled with one of each thing. Marianne buys one of each too: one potato, one tomato, one lime, one chunk of ginger root, one apple, one peach, one sprig of rosemary, one bagel. She brings it all home and sets it on the kitchen counter, photographs it, sends Felix the pictures. My supper, she writes. He doesn't text back.

12

Marianne is in bed, bleeding in her ballerina dress. She fell asleep in it, thinking of you, Felix. The dress is ruined and still more blood comes, and Marianne soaks up wads of toilet paper that she has jammed between her legs. She wishes she could fall asleep again, but she can't. She has to go out to mail a package to Felix, a pair of gloves. He will be on the shoot one extra week.

On the way to the postal office, Marianne feels something slide down her leg and once she crosses the street, she ducks inside an elementary school on the corner and she goes to the bathroom, where she reaches into the pant leg and pulls out a snail-like, gelatinous thing. She takes a picture of it against a soft bed of toilet paper — it now exists next to the picture of the organic apple that she photographed the day before — and then she flushes it down the toilet.

The next day, Marianne goes to see her family doctor. The doctor examines the picture of the organic apple until Marianne realizes her mistake and swipes over to the red thing. The doctor squints. That looks like an air sac.

The doctor sends Marianne for tests. Marianne tests positive.

She calls Felix that evening and she doesn't know how to tell him so that she doesn't seem like a psycho who's tried to trap him with a baby — or whatever people think of women early in relationships getting knocked up — so she laughs and she apologizes, she doesn't know why she's even telling him, it's not like anything happened, in fact a thing *un*happened, it's not like she even knew she was pregnant, she is in her forties, what are the chances, she laughs and at the end of it she actually has no idea if he even understood what she just told him, he sounds so nonplussed.

The doctor asks Marianne to keep doing the tests and Marianne goes one more time, the test says < 4, which is a positive phantom.

It occurs to Marianne that the young guy she slept with, Eric, was possibly the father, with his ten-years-younger sperm, and she doesn't text Felix to come home sooner just because she's starting to feel funny, or sad — sad-funny, actually.

13

They break up a few weeks later, in the middle of the night.

Marianne waits for the morning light to wash over Felix's studio so that she can memorize the place where she's been most happy and the least hungry. Felix is lying next to her with his eyes open.

How do you feel? she asks.

Hollow, he says.

Marianne cannot think of a worse way to feel. She herself doesn't feel hollow or full; she feels painfully hungry, but not for me.

She gets up and walks around the apartment, picking up pieces of herself: a toothbrush, an earring, a book, a coffee mug, a pamphlet from a mall announcing a new Italian restaurant. Felix is in bed, the blankets pulled over his legs. Marianne doesn't move fast.

She thinks of the time they went to visit his friends on the island when he came back from the shoot, how much fun they had in a car for the first hour and a half, and how frightfully angry he seemed when she got out of the ferry bathroom too soon: Did you even wash your hands?

Later, he asked her again about the tattoo on her back — was it a flower or some kind of an artichoke or what? He was holding on to her hips as he went in and out of her. They were renting a room in an empty for-sale hotel, right next to his friend's little cottage house. At night, they both lay stiffly, trying not to move but above all trying not to fart, their stomachs grumbling from the terrible Tibetan food they had eaten before sleep. The next day they skated, shot videos of themselves in the snow, and fucked in the hotel, their stomachs empty of me. Marianne thought all the badness had passed.

That was three weeks ago. This is now and Felix does nothing, says nothing. He's leaving for another shoot soon. Marianne feels cheated, not of him or even the baby but of grief because how do you grieve something you didn't know was possible?

When she gets home, she orders all the comforting softness of me, blankets and blankets of dough to bury herself under in dumplings, and croissants, and pastas, and creamy sweetness of sauces.

14

It is true that when Marianne first read about this method of having all of me, she imagined this unfortunate possibility; she had imagined herself with her face shattered against bathroom tiles white like her teeth, her cheek next to the slick holiness of a toilet, her eyes bulging, her ugly glasses askew.

But I am gentle as I block Marianne's passages, although she dislocates her right shoulder when she tries to empty herself of me one last time. She hits herself in the chest with her left fist as I expand and fill her, mercifully, all that empty space where the love was, where the non-baby isn't. I am comfort and I am peace and she never has to worry again about what I could do to her body because now I do the only thing that is irreversible as she collapses onto the floor.

LORENZO AND THE LAST FIG

Eddy Boudel Tan

Everyone was tired. It might have been the smothering heat of that August morning, or perhaps the smoke that was said to be coming from the mainland like an all-consuming shadow, that made their limbs heavy and their thoughts adrift. They huddled beneath the café's awning with cups in their hands and no attempts to stir the stillness. Even when the cry came from the edge of town, a sharp and wobbly sound that might have struck them as urgent in another time, they simply subdued the rumble of dread in their bellies and waited.

Little Willow appeared from around the corner, a strange girl with a helmet of black hair and wide, intense eyes. Seconds of silence, long enough to refill her lungs with hiccups of dusty air. "You won't bel—" she managed to say before the inevitable interruption.

"Willow Hasegawa," said a man beneath the wide brim of a hat. He had a ghostly face, with sunken cheeks rarely touched by the sun. "What're you hollering for?"

She stepped into the awning's merciful shade. "You won't believe what I just found." Stares and silence all around her. "In the forest," she explained further.

"What," said a woman with an exhausted slouch in her shoulders, "in the world did you see?"

Willow coaxed them with a wave of the hand. "Follow me."

Some couldn't be bothered to endure the heat for what might have been a girl's silly game, but curiosity had been piqued for most. They abandoned their cups of murky darkness, trudging across the asphalt toward the allure of the forest. Sure-footed and with a whiff of authority, Willow led the way around scarred trunks and ancient roots.

She came to a stop so abrupt the line of adults behind her compressed with bumped limbs and a chorus of "sorry." Her arms were stretched to the side, palms up, as if revealing something divine.

It was a tree, unlike any other tree on their twenty-square-kilometre, moss-covered rock in the Salish Sea. In contrast to the giants that towered over them, its meagre body formed a trident of ashen bark that stood only double Willow's height. The branches held floppy leaves shaped like continents, a brighter shade of green than they were accustomed to seeing. A moment passed before anyone noticed the bulbs hidden between the leaves.

"Well, I'll be," said the man in the hat.

The others voiced similar sentiments, their words melding together in collective confusion.

"What is it?" demanded the woman with the exhausted shoulders.

All eyes turned to little Willow, and she shrugged. A soft voice rose from within the crowd, at waist height.

"Fichi." The voice belonged to a boy nobody had noticed was among them. In fact, nobody knew much about him at all, even though a full year had passed since he and his aunt had arrived on the island. They came from Italy, a place many of the locals romanticized as resembling the images they'd seen a quarter-century ago. Lorenzo was eleven or twelve, short for his age, with chestnut hair that crested at the top like an ocean's wave.

Lorenzo saw the blankness in their eyes, then reached into his growing reservoir of English. "Fig," he said. "It is a fig tree, with fig fruit."

Their astonishment was audible because they realized he was right. The older ones remembered a time when figs could be grown even in their corner of the world, before most of Earth's fruit withered into memory. Sigatoka, it was called, a malevolent fungus that had come for bananas first, then mangos and papayas. Chemicals couldn't keep it at bay, its many strains accelerating alongside the temperatures and humidity that fuelled them. Before long, most of the world's fruit crops were blackened by rot, and it became too costly to do much about it. By then, synthetic vitamins were rather effective and genetically engineered apples plentiful.

Children marvelled at old images of the world's lost fruit — such whimsical shapes and colours — while the older generations lamented them. They longed to taste the delicate sweetness, feel the stickiness between their fingers. Most humans hadn't touched a real fig — or grape or lemon or plum, for that matter — since 2036.

"Stand back," bellowed the ghostly man in the hat. His eyes sharpened as he inspected the fruit, while his hands resisted the urge to reach out and touch. "Healthy," he said, seeing no evidence of the rusty wounds in its leaves that were signs of Sigatoka. He turned to face the small and patient crowd. "We must notify Council. In the meantime, nobody lays a finger on this tree. You hear?" Nods all around. "Rahim," he said, pointing to a man wearing a similar style of hat. "Stay behind. Make sure nobody comes near."

With that, everyone but Rahim retreated toward town, the ghost-faced man assuming the lead.

Lorenzo unhooked a cap from his belt loop and placed it on his head. It was a size or so too large, but it fit loosely over his thick heap of hair. He lagged behind, feeling no urgency to return to the malaise of town. He preferred the shifting shadows of the forest, the sun-bleached driftwood of pebbly coves.

Nothing about this island reminded him of Italy, though. His memory was shaped like ancient paths that wound across barren hills. Green was a forgotten colour, yet there had been trees in his mother's garden, a small cluster of fichi — figs — that rose tenaciously from the soil.

When he was younger, he hadn't realized how special they were, how remarkably rare. They were hidden behind a stone wall that encircled their house. He pictured the roof of terracotta tiles, an earthy shade beneath the relentless sun, and shutters painted the colour of basil. He imagined the little mole below his mother's left eye, heard her laughter, which sounded more like the growl of a bear than the song of a bird. A feeling of loss pierced something deep within his chest, and he pushed aside the memories of moles and terracotta and fig trees.

"I like your hat," said Willow, sidling up beside him.

He took it off his head to have a look, as if he'd forgotten. Black with a curved bill. Embroidered on the front was a red cross and stripes beneath the letters *ACM*.

"Thank you," he said. "It belonged to my brother."

Willow's face scrunched up. "You never said you had a brother."

"His name is Matteo." He tucked his hair back into the cap, hoping Willow wouldn't press any further. The girl seemed to understand and offered a comforting silence by his side.

The humid air swallowed them as they stepped out of the forest and into town. Light sparkled along rooftop solar panels, brilliantly blinding. The streets were busier now, locals running errands despite the heat. Even with the brightly painted buildings and sunshine, Lorenzo found it to be a dreary place, a facade for the pervasive weariness that emanated from its older citizens. People in orange uniforms held thick hoses like anacondas, spraying sea water onto the trees along the forest's edge. The rains were missed, and everyone feared the wind that was said to carry smoke and embers from the mainland.

"Lorenzo!" His aunt, Benedetta, waved at him from a table beneath the café's awning.

He turned to Willow and said, "I have to go," but she was already walking away with a smile and two fingers pointed like rabbit ears.

A lovely sprinkle of Italian sounds escaped Aunt Benedetta's lips, but she stopped herself, glancing side to side to see if anyone on the patio had noticed, then began again in her second language. "Where have you been hiding, little mouse? Remember, we have guests coming for supper tonight. The Zarbs." Her eyes swept across the other tables to detect whether they'd heard her mention the respected couple.

Lorenzo took the seat across from her and nodded. Benedetta and his mother had always been different, even though they were sisters only three years apart, but the disparity had widened after Benedetta and Lorenzo arrived in Canada. She'd always been the flashy one, relishing attention in all its crude forms, while his mother was plain and happily unmemorable. Canada had given Benedetta a new social mountain to climb — a steep one, considering the status they'd received. The fashions here were bright and indulgent, a welcome contrast to the austerity of Europe, and Benedetta embraced it all as if she'd already laid her homeland to rest.

She took a sip from her cup, and her smile soured at the taste — coffee beans were another lost delicacy, unattainable to all but the very wealthy. The synthetic-hybrid reincarnation made a poor substitute for those who remembered the richness of a warm espresso.

"I'm making your favourite tonight," she said. "Cacio e pepe."

Lorenzo smiled at the thought of swirled noodles drenched in oil, buried beneath generous coats of black pepper and freshly grated pecorino. The taste was of home.

A smouldering fog rolled over the island that evening, an unwelcome gift from the easterly winds. The locals had been anticipating it for weeks, and the encroaching darkness could be seen on the other side of the Salish Sea that blue-skied morning. Now, land and sea and sky were obscured by smoke, tinted a hazy shade of orange by the descending sun.

Even so, the locals were grateful. Better the smoke than the fires.

Lorenzo and Benedetta lived in a small house made of concrete columns and sheet metal. Benedetta had done her best to make it a home, framing photographs for the walls and decorating the sofas with an abundance of cushions, but home was not how it felt.

A knock on the door came ten minutes too early. "Madonna mia," Benedetta muttered, still applying the final touches to the table setting. "These people do not understand good manners."

Lorenzo straightened the dining chairs as Benedetta tossed her apron into the pantry. She gave herself a once-over in the mirror before opening the door with her most charming smile, greeting her guests with the local custom of a palm against her heart.

An incendiary scent wafted into the house as Mr. and Mrs. Zarb shuffled inside with boisterous voices and the occasional cough.

"We brought a Lloyd salad," the woman said, placing a bowl into Benedetta's unsuspecting hands.

"How kind," she replied, though Lorenzo could hear the distaste beneath the words.

Before long, they were seated around the dining table, scooping Lloyd salad onto their plates even though Benedetta had prepared multiple courses. Lorenzo stared at the pile of root vegetables, cubed and tossed with dill and a mustardy mayonnaise, that lay in front of him. He placed a cube into his mouth and tried not to grimace.

Mrs. Zarb sat on Island Council, while her husband had something to do with coordinating shipments of supplies from the mainland. They both had small eyes behind large spectacles, and lips so pale it was difficult to discern where they ended or began. They consumed the salad as if competing against the clock, then washed it down with gulps of apple wine.

Mrs. Zarb wiped her lips before asking, "Have you heard about the fig tree?"

Benedetta responded that she had not, while Lorenzo stayed quiet.

"A real fig tree, with real figs, in the forest by Yaro Bay. Willow Hasegawa discovered it. Can you believe it?"

Benedetta's eyes widened. "They are healthy, the figs? We can eat them?"

Mrs. Zarb laughed, an unpleasant sound that came from deep within her nasal cavity. "Perhaps, darling," she said. "We're discussing how to handle the situation at Council, but for now it's being guarded. So, we'll see."

Once the plates were cleared, Lorenzo wondered if Benedetta would skip the first course she'd planned, since back-to-back salads might have been excessive, but she was undeterred. It wasn't quite the Caprese salad she'd grown up eating, but she had to work with what she could acquire: greenhouse tomatoes that were modified to withstand Sigatoka, "mozzarella" from Canadian cows rather than buffalo, and local basil that tasted like grass. All of it was drizzled in synthetic olive oil, a tangy syrup that appeared duller than the real thing despite being an unnaturally vibrant shade of yellow.

Mr. and Mrs. Zarb oohed and aahed at the presentation, an abstract and edible Italian flag against white porcelain. They placed forkfuls into their mouths and savoured the flavours, unlike how they'd eaten the Lloyd salad.

"Did you know," Mrs. Zarb said, her lips twisted in delight, "that we travelled to Italy on our honeymoon? Twenty-five years ago."

"Twenty-six," Mr. Zarb corrected. "We were married in 2023, love."

"Right," she said with an impatient flutter of fingers. "But, wow, what a marvellous place. Stunning, just stunning. We drank Aperol spritzes every evening. The palazzos in Venice — such elegance, even with the laundry strung up to dry. And we ate our way through Tuscany, didn't we, dear?" He nodded, and she continued. "Truffles and hazelnuts and so much gelato! We drove from village to village, past cypress trees and olive groves. It was everything we'd dreamed it would be."

She paused for a breath, a zealous sparkle in her eyes that made her appear slightly unhinged, as she gazed past their shoulders. Then she seemed to remember where she was and reeled herself back in.

Leaning toward her hosts, she said, "You are both very lucky to come from that splendid place."

Lorenzo dropped his fork and knife onto his plate. "What place?" he said. "What is this splendid, marvellous place you speak of?"

Mrs. Zarb straightened in her seat, her eyebrows arched high above her spectacles.

"It does not exist," he went on. "Not anymore. Venice is underwater, the palazzi not very elegant in the sea. The olives have all died. The cypress trees burned."

"Topolino," said Benedetta to her nephew, but that was the extent of her weary protest.

Lorenzo ignored her. "The truffles and hazelnuts and gelato — no more! All gone because of people like you. People who take, take, take, without thinking or caring. So you are wrong, Mrs. Zarb. We are not lucky, because our home, our real home, is unlivable."

"I —" Mrs. Zarb began to say, but her husband silenced her with a gentle hand on her lap.

Lorenzo stood and placed his napkin on the table. "Excuse me," he said in a quiet voice. He retreated into his bedroom, co-cooned himself inside his blanket, and remembered his mother.

———————

She had been a hopeful woman. Even as the land around her decayed, she maintained a refuge of comfort, of calm, within the stone walls of her home, a vital oasis in the scorched hills outside Siena. Lorenzo was brought into a world of drought and famine, but there was also music from his mother's acoustic guitar as she sang "Amori Infiniti" like a lullaby, games played with dice and tattered cards, laughter. So much laughter, usually sparked by Matteo's jokes, his ridiculous antics.

Their mother's walled garden concealed an abundance of treasures: squash and arugula and radicchio, nourished during the dry months from well water and love. The figs were always Lorenzo's favourite. Every summer he'd watch as the figs transformed from emeralds to amethysts. He'd stretch his little hands to the sky, unable to reach, until his mother would lift him by the waist so he could grasp them.

"Do not tell anyone about this fruit," his mother would say, kneeling low so their eyes were level. "It is our secret."

He'd nod, uncomprehending their rareness until he was older. During their last spring together, he asked her how it was possible this fruit could grow while all the others had died years before.

"I protect them," she said.

She picked a handful of painted daisies that grew along the garden wall. She ground them in her mortar, then added a generous pour of sunflower oil and amaro. After transferring the mixture into a bottle, she led Lorenzo into the garden. She spritzed the trees with the amber liquid as the lyrics of "Amori Infiniti" rose and fell from her lips.

"This is the most important part," she said at the end. "The tree must know it is loved."

———

Smoke settled into the atmosphere above the island in the days that followed, and the sun became a fiery spectre behind the haze.

Word of the fig tree had spread like ashes in the wind. The entire island was talking about the miraculous fruit, and they speculated what its appearance must mean. Was it a sign of hope, of an ecological renaissance? Or would it rot like the others before it, or worse, bring new waves of infectious devastation?

Island Council decided to establish a perimeter around the tree, ten metres wide and guarded around the clock. They cleared the moss that carpeted the forest floor until the fig tree was alone in the centre of a barren circle. It drew crowds of on-lookers, some coming to worship as if it were the Virgin Mary crying tears of blood.

On the fourth day, Lorenzo sprinted between the ever-greens and through the lingering smoke. His feet leaped over boulders and roots, his throat itching. He arrived at the clear-ing and saw it was true, what he'd heard. Men in orange suits were installing a chain-link fence along the perimeter that had been cleared for the fig tree. The tangle of metal rose high above his head, more an instrument of control than protection. He peered through the diamond-shaped openings in the fence and could feel the tree's sadness. Its leaves were limper and a paler shade of green, yearning to touch something other than ash in the air. Lorenzo squinted, and worry seized him by the chest when he saw the skin of the figs had taken on a bruise-like shade of purple. They were beginning to ripen.

"Draconian, isn't it?" The voice came from behind, and he spun around to see Willow Hasegawa. She was dressed in candy colours, with faux bunny ears pointing upward from the headband in her hair.

"Draccordion?"

"It's silly," she said, "and extreme. I mean, it's fruit! We should be eating it, and taking the seeds and planting them to make more fruit. Instead, they're guarding it like the Pope."

"The Pope is gone," he said. "And that's not the best way."

"Huh?"

"Seeds," Lorenzo said. "The trees grow slower from the seeds. It is better to take pieces of the tree — the little branches, yes? — and put them in the soil. These pieces grow roots, then become trees."

"Oh," Willow said, surprised by this new knowledge.

There was a starry and distant glint in Lorenzo's drifting eyes. "And the most important part is this: The tree must know it is loved."

———

The fence around the fig tree reminded him of the port in Livorno. Closed gates and impenetrable barriers. Floodlights and uniformed men with large guns. It was a memory that stung his eyes even now, a year later.

His life had felt ordinary only months before Livorno, despite the devastation all around him from an historic absence of rain. Even as talk of evacuation began to intensify among neighbours, Lorenzo had never felt unsafe.

But then Benedetta fled her apartment in Florence, leaving everything behind except her passport and a handbag filled with jewellery. Lorenzo had never seen her so distressed, lines and dirt streaked across her face where there was normally colour. She barged through the front door in a frenzy of noise and movement, telling them they must leave. His mother guided Benedetta into a chair, tried calming her with a glass of amaro.

"The city is under siege," Benedetta explained. Thousands were migrating north, flooding into Rome, Florence, Milan. She described mass encampments throughout the Boboli Gardens, riots in Piazza della Repubblica. Doctors were tending to the sick beneath Brunelleschi's six-century-old dome, the cathedral now a makeshift hospital. Home invasions were becoming common as desperation took hold, and the once-stubborn Florentines were now fleeing the city for safety in the hills.

Of course, they'd heard the stories coming from all corners of Italy, but Lorenzo's mother hadn't realized it was so dire.

"Houses in the countryside are being raided," Benedetta said, her voice trembling. "You aren't safe here."

At first, Lorenzo's mother didn't respond. Their home had survived drought and wildfire. They'd sung and laughed and grown despite the danger that surrounded them. Were they fools to believe it could go on?

She turned to Lorenzo and Matteo, and they knew not to argue by one look at her face. "Pack one bag each," she said. "Bring only what you cannot live without."

On the seventh day after the tree was discovered, Island Council held a public meeting at the hall. People argued over what to do with the tree. Some demanded that the fruit be harvested and eaten, while others made a case for using pieces of the tree to plant more. Neither side seemed to realize they could do both.

Lorenzo wanted to speak up and point this out, but then the ghostly man with the wide hat stood from the front row and cried, "Science!" This caught everyone's attention and, quite pleased with himself, he went on. "We don't know where this tree came from or how it's remained healthy. We must study it."

There was a pause, then a rumble of affirmation. "Brilliant idea," they said. "We must study it," they repeated as if the idea were theirs.

Island Council sent word to the provincial capital, and a team of arborists, botanists, climatologists, and epidemiologists was assembled. More days passed, and the locals waited.

Lorenzo visited the tree every morning, when the smoke seemed thinner and the ground was soft with dew. He would sit on a mound of moss and peer through the chain-link fence, pretending he didn't notice the guard watching him. The tree was heavy with loneliness. How could it feel loved when it was secluded and patrolled, cut off from all other life? Rather than reaching for the sky, its leaves bowed to the bare soil. The fruits were plump, though, and Lorenzo knew they would soon rot. They were meant to be plucked and savoured, their juice dripping from mouths in trails that sparkled in sunlight, not examined like specimens in a lab.

On the thirteenth day, the fruits were gone. Council had been so focused on keeping the humans away, they hadn't thought much about the birds that weren't deterred by tall fences. Lorenzo was glad the fruits were enjoyed before they soured.

By the time the team of scientists arrived on shore, the tree's leaves were beginning to show signs of weakness. They couldn't say for certain it was Sigatoka, but nevertheless the locals mourned the loss of what they had once believed was special. Most of all, they felt a familiar pang in their chests, a mixture of shame and disappointment that was too often the result of hope. But it felt good to hope, even if only temporarily, and so they would allow themselves to hope again.

Lorenzo hid in the shadows of the forest, watching the scientists dismember the lonely tree. They sawed off its branches and dug up its roots, placing the pieces into plastic bags. Soon, all that was left was a hole surrounded by a fence.

"Positively Kafkaesque."

Lorenzo turned to see Willow Hasegawa, dressed like a Victorian doll at a funeral.

"Kafka-what?"

"This," she said, pointing at the newly formed hole in the ground. "We had something beautiful and rare, and they chopped it into kindling."

The girl's conviction made him laugh.

"It's not funny," she said as she took a seat beside him. "That might have been the last fig tree on Earth."

Lorenzo looked at her with a sad smile. "Those trees grew in our garden, in the house where I lived with my mother and brother. I think there must be more, out there, somewhere."

Willow glanced at the black cap on Lorenzo's head. "What happened to them?" she asked. "I mean, your mother and brother?"

"We were forced to leave our home during the second great drought," Lorenzo said. "My aunt found a way for us to come to Canada, for asylum. We were supposed to come here together."

His breath caught in his throat at the memory of Livorno — throngs of jostling elbows and grasping hands, the scent of desperation heavy in the air, of sweat and soil. He could hear their cries, feel the floodlights blinding his eyes. The ship at the dock had seemed unreachably far, a gauntlet of gates and guards between them. His mother's hand had gripped his like a vise, while his other hand was secured around the strap of his backpack. They inched closer, winding through the crowd as his mother and aunt held their chins high. Finally, they reached an officer standing at the first gate. Benedetta thrust papers into his hands, and it felt like they'd made it.

Willow waited for him to go on, but his gaze had drifted to the forest floor. She steeled herself and asked, "Why aren't they here?"

"Because of Matteo," he said. "My brother. He had some trouble with the police when he was younger, stealing this from a shop." Waves of hair spilled from beneath his cap as he held it before him. "It was a stupid mistake, but it followed him. They would not let him on the boat, so we separated. My aunt took me, and my mother and brother stayed behind."

Lorenzo could hear his mother's hopeful voice as she pleaded with the officer to let Matteo through. A flicker of vulnerability, of compassion, had passed across the officer's eyes, and for a second they believed in humanity, that this man would never split a family apart. Then he blinked, and they realized they should have known better.

Lorenzo's screams eclipsed his mother's as Benedetta pulled him forward by the hand. "Come," she demanded, but he didn't want to go with her. He wrenched himself free from Benedetta's grip and pushed through the crowd, toward his mother and brother.

"You must go," his mother had begged him when he reached the gate. "Please, Lorenzo, listen to me. Go with your aunt, and we will see you soon. You cannot stay here."

His vision had been so blurry with tears he couldn't see how his mother looked in that moment. Yet the scent of her hair and skin imprinted itself in his memory, the aroma of almonds and flowers and figs.

Before Lorenzo could protest, Matteo shoved his favourite black cap into his shaking hands. "Look after this for me," Matteo had said.

When Lorenzo's eyes were able to focus through the tears and floodlights, they were gone.

"That's awful," Willow said, clutching the fabric of her dress.

Lorenzo sensed what she was too polite, or frightened, to ask. "They are safe, my mother and brother. They went north, over the mountains." He paused, wondering what they were doing in that moment on the other side of the world. "We are trying to bring them here, but it is not simple."

Willow's face brightened, but only slightly. "We'll find a way," she said, placing a gentle hand on his knee, and his loneliness faded a shade.

"Want to see a secret?" he asked, strapping on his backpack.

"Sure. I've heard secrets before, but I'm not sure I've ever *seen* one."

Lorenzo shot to his feet, and Willow followed. They darted through the forest, down ravines and along winding creeks. The smoke had finally cleared that morning, and their lungs ballooned with untainted oxygen. Willow sounded out of breath when Lorenzo slowed at the top of a ridge. He led her down a path that was barely there, into a glade that was sheltered by evergreens. Sunlight spilled through the canopy overhead in shape-shifting patterns on the grass.

Willow's mouth widened when she saw five slender trees, arranged like the points of a star in the glade's centre. They were shorter and thinner than the tree that had caused such commotion, and there was no fruit dangling from the branches, but clearly they were figs by their floppy leaves and ashen bark.

"I told you," said Lorenzo, "that the best way to grow a fig is by planting branches instead of seeds. Well, these came from pieces of the trees from my mother's garden. Before we left our home, she told me and Matteo to pack only what we could not live without."

Willow approached one tree, breathing in the scent of its bark. "You brought these with you, from Italy?"

"I did not know if the branches would survive," he admitted. "I planted the first one closer to town, the day after we arrived. It started to grow, and so I planted these a few weeks later. That first one was special — the fruit should have taken years to appear." He ran his fingers along the veins of the leaves, allowing himself to feel a little sadness for that lonely tree. "These are growing more slowly, but they are healthy."

"How is it possible? These trees went extinct years ago."

Lorenzo reached into his backpack, pulling out a glass bottle that had once held perfume. He sprayed the trees with the potion he'd learned: crushed daisies with cooking oil and a drizzle of amaro. Soon, the leaves glistened and the air smelled like his mother.

"This is the most important part," he whispered. "The tree must know it is loved."

With that, he began to sing in a language that felt at once immortal and ephemeral, as if time were made meaningless by its sound. His voice rose and fell, through the stillness of the forest, and Willow cried tears of grief, and of wonder, and of hope.

FOOD FIGHT

Chris Benjamin

OBSIDIAN

'll tell you what's wrong with this situation. Thousands of
Island farmers blocking Route 1 right near Confederation
Bridge — may it crumble into the sea — with our tractors
like we done in the 1970s and again in the 2020s and expecting this time it'll bring MacEnDish to their knees like it never
done the first two times. Like we can match might with might.

The tactics are fine — it's not that. We found the right place
to make a bottleneck and it'll soon be a flashpoint and it'll flash
all right, brighter than the Point Lighthouse when they blew
it up in '27. Problem is it'll be us up in flames. These other
farmers don't think a company will get violent. Somebody must
have dropped them on their heads.

Sawyer says we been burning ever since the first food raid.
At first we took them as we saw them: hungry neighbours
running off with root vegetables in the night, shadows in the

dark, making light sounds and subtle sights, rustling leaves and stalks swaying against the backdrop of the heavy harvest moon. We shut off the sprinklers so in the morning's muck we could trace hardened outlines of thrift-store runners. You could tell by the uneven depths of their impressions, made by old shoes worn in by some individual's idiosyncratic steps over many years. The wearer of such castaways was desperate, as if their nighttime thieving wasn't indication enough.

Sawyer scoffed at my sleuthing deductions, said I read too many old-timey whodunits.

"You ain't read enough anything," I barked. If only their mother had stuck around — Jean loved literature and when Jean loved something, it was contagious.

Anyway, Sawyer one-upped me, ran a scanner over the runner prints and declared them synthetic. "Robotic," that is. A simulacrum of human crime. "You know things are bad when the robots raid the farm disguised as vagrants."

"Maybe they're trying to make us turn on our neighbours, sow a little division like."

After that they sent a unit every month or so, always at night, until last month Sawyer blew it to cybernetic bits of plastic with a gun they printed using an old design they got online. My child frightens me sometimes. I swept away the pieces with the push broom. I don't know what might happen next. That is what is wrong with the situation.

Mine is one of the last productive farms on the Island, and it gives me the daily hymnal of watching sun-cast coral hues over scattered pumpkins and rows of green roughage, or the glistening jagged edges of hemp, depending on the season. It's been organic my whole life. Thank Angus for that; my father was one of them back-to-the-land hiphoppers and he sent me to agricultural college to be smarter about the operation than his trial-by-error. Now here's me and Sawyer fighting off sneaky simulacra with artillery they made from their computer on the 3-D printer.

What they're really after, I think, is the seeds, which we keep banked — five of each variety — in a rusty cistern down in the old pipe system from when we had a proper government providing for us certain infrastructural needs like running water. Had to dig a few hours deep to find the right spot. MacEnDish could seize the land and let it go to seed, I suppose, but they've got just enough lingering respect for the Crown that was, and the old ways, and they'd rather not look like robber barons marching us off our deeded land. That's what's wrong with this situation: we're forcing their hand when we could just sit tight, keep growing our own, the few of us left with arable land. But the others are antsy, and Sawyer's eager to use their weaponry. I hope it doesn't come to that. We just want to make a statement — me and the other old-timey farmers getting repeatedly raided. Just want to cut off the potato export for a few hours, cost them some money the same way they cost us. Let them know we won't just roll over. But it's dangerous.

When MacEnDish merged and took ownership of the Island, Angus refused to sell. He was one of the stubborn few and in no time we went from five thousand farms to just a few dozen, the holdouts and potato monolith squeezing us out. The cousins were on Angus fierce to cave when their offer hit seven figures, more than he'd made in a lifetime of planting complementary foods. But all those millionaires were the same ones now stealing vegetables from our solar greenhouse-slash-water-filtration system. We have a potluck with them when we have extra — contributions optional.

"We plant it, we grow it, we harvest it, we sell it, and we goddamn eat it," Angus thundered back in the day. He was one who enjoyed a good hard rant. "It's ours, goddamn it!"

He meant the food, but not just the hardy vegetables. He started this clever system of flint corn, beans, and squash, though he insisted he learned it from his friend Jenni, who claimed to be an Aztec. I think she got it from a book. We learned similar stuff in our permaculture course at the college. Corn leaches nitrogen from the soil. It mixes up with the beans, which naturally replenish nitrogen. Squash gives off some water and its leaves block sunlight to weeds. So those three things help each other out. Complementary. I grow thirty different vegetables here and yes, we do help hungry neighbours when we can and no, MacEnDish don't like it.

The bottleneck we're creating, blocking MacEnDish's trucks full of synthetic potatoes, is also what is wrong. I'm not sure how they'll respond, but I have heard rumours they have built a fleet of super-robots, made as overscale replicas of twentieth-century toys some CEO remembered fondly, but featuring articulated sensory heads and hydraulically activated joints or some such nonsense voodoo that makes them super-humanly fast, agile, and accurate even at fifty storeys in height, and loaded with small-scale nuclear weapons. The problem is even Sawyer's submachine guns would be sticks and stones to them, four-letter words at best.

What's worse, I hear MacEnDish has trained the things to do a victory dance after they kill. They of course don't know that's what they are doing. They will trample our rusted twentieth-century tractors and our ninth-century fields and dance upon our shallow modern graves, unaware of the artistry in any of it. They can't know the beauty of one form of life meeting the needs of another as the other meets the needs of a third, which meets the needs of the first. Each piece of machinery will dance alone and know not even a molecule of sorrow for what it lacks.

My cousin Isabel should know these things, but they replaced her organic matter with sensors and wiring at law school, and she asks me to this day why I must be so much like my father, why I can't be more like other farmers. Her Mercedes overtakes my tractor on the other side of the double line on Route 1, speeding to beat the tractors to the site — I know some will already be there — her horn tooting "Achy Breaky Heart" as she waves. Her husband is with her in the passenger seat, and in the back is her pale-skinned son and her demented father, who stares at his hands. I point to the roadside potato gallery, the toothless, slumped-over, and crooked-limbed holding their signs with shaky pink hands: "GIB US UR STROW BEARYS" and "SHAR UR WATER." One gestures pathetically to his mouth with his fingers.

I shout to Isabel, "Should I be more like them?" but she can't hear and she wouldn't understand. I don't hate her, though — not like Sawyer does. Family's family. Besides, Sawyer's more like Isabel than they realize, with all their faith in technology, as if it doesn't amplify human greed. Sawyer's the only possible future, though, so I hope they know what they're doing.

SAWYER

Sawyer knows this much: if you could harvest and compost people's bullshit, you might actually salvage this cracked-sand desert moonscape. Problem is it would take some sort of technological innovation to transform claptrap into kilowatts, and the oldhead farmers are not exactly what you'd call early adopters. Sawyer's father still raves on about how his father, Sawyer's grandfather, was ahead of his time because he planted more than one type of seed, like Grandpa Angus was Newton and dirt farming was gravity. Yet anything derived by an algorithm is Obsidian's enemy. As if technology isn't controlled by human hands. As if the seeds he stubbornly claims ownership over aren't themselves technology.

Isabel, the Vantablack sheep of the family, legal counsel for MacEnDish Atlantic, may have stumbled upon a kernel of truth when she said Obsidian was too long deprived of a woman's pleasure and had fallen in love with the surrogate past. Then again, Isabel and her husband couldn't be bothered to care for their own. Their son, Aiden, is a cyberterrorist and their demented father, Landon, wanders around downtown, groping unsuspecting young women who absent-mindedly let him get close enough to reach. "Young ladies," he calls them. He tried that shit on Sawyer once and they hope he still has the bruise. Whatever Sawyer is, it ain't a lady. Landon and Aiden were both permanent residents on Sawyer's list of stupids, which they dictate to their screen as they bounce in the driver's seat of the tractor, which pulls a trailer loaded with foldable machine guns they printed at home:

Sawyer Arseneault's List of Stupids

1. Counter-protestors who can't spell. Yes they're
   desperate and so I can't hate 'em and I must
   pity 'em but dog damn me I don't even barely
   read except online, and I can spell "strawberry."

1B. [Sawyer clearly needs to build their
empathy muscle because they feel only
contempt watching these people, poor
and emaciated, hands out, mouths opening and closing. Maybe if they hadn't
sealed their own fates being greedy,
back before Sawyer was born. Obsidian
stays up nights worrying about them,
their pain, the likelihood it will drive
them to destroy his house or torture the
location of the master seeds from him.
Sawyer reassures him they don't have the
energy for that, and it is the MacEnDish
he has to worry about, and he waves
Sawyer away like they are a child. Maybe
Obsidian prefers worrying about the
helpless and dishevelled to worrying
about what MacEnDish will do to them
if it can't find his original seeds.]

2. Kids who quit. The ones who go away, as
if elsewhere is really different, and all they
really want is to get laid outside their own
gene pool. I mean, just be honest about that.
Reasonable enough. But the ones who act
like missionaries out to save unfortunates or
economic mercenaries with stakes to claim
in some exotic land that still has ice, leaving
home to crumble and burn. "Elsewhere is
burned stew flung far away," Grandpa Angus
used to say. Something like that. Burned, all

right. Everything burning, but at least have the cojones to stay and fight.

2B. [As for sexing outside the gene pool, it's a nice thought but we're all connected back to Africa. Anyway, Sawyer takes care of their own needs, and technology helps them with that too.]

3. As for economic exile, judging from the go-aways' posts, they're just staking claim on a different pile of the same problems: debt and shortages and terrible weather.

3B. [Sawyer makes plenty of money selling 3-D print designs for low-carbon machinery — they can buy anything they want from endless aisles of canned goods, different pictures but the contents are all the same, different words but the mush inside tastes identical. Sawyer doesn't feel great about charging for what they know is available elsewhere, for free, open source, if people had the brains to do their research. But at least the designs aren't corporate owned.]

4. And Sawyer's stupid crush on their stupid cousin, Aiden, the little dweeb. Speaking of gene pool challenges. Aiden ArsenHole, who

talked Sawyer into sharing a shot of their junk, then posted it with an anonymous account and a disgusting caption questioning their gender choices while also insulting their genitalia.

5. The dozens of stupid people who misspelled so-gross comments on Aiden's post of Sawyer's junk. It's also possible Aiden created dozens of profiles and made all the misspellings himself. In person he's such a sweet little nothing, five-foot-one and the son of a lawyer and a librarian (who's totally closeted). Sawyer never thought he had the cojones.

6. Obsidian Arsenault, who raves about the artistry of the seeds, their tremendous ability to complement one another, supplement one another, "care for" one another's needs, yet fails to appreciate the artistry of the machines, how a mathematical theory even goes by the name "complement," how components of a well-designed machine act exactly like a community, helping one another out (in ways humans rarely do anymore), not only carrying out their own roles but emitting by-products (excess fluids, converted gases) that then get sucked up as inputs into the same machine. In this way, before Obsidian's very eyes, Sawyer made a solar water purification system that is home to diverse bacteria and plants and fish, right inside the greenhouses.

They use it to feed the sprinklers and water
crops in times of general shortage, sometimes
filling buckets for their neighbours.

Sawyer arrives in good time, pulling in behind another
tractor to complete a third row across the highway. They em-
brace their father and the other farmers and their children
and in some cases grandchildren. Someone has already set
up a small, black riser stage and podium behind the tractors.
Sawyer scans 360 degrees — no sign of security yet. They
unstrap and haul down the crate of weapons from the flatbed
trailer behind their red tractor. The trailer is overkill; there
are only a couple of dozen guns, each of which folds up nicely
into a shoebox. It's just a stack of shoeboxes, from which the
rectangular plastic device can be unfolded and strapped over
a shoulder and fired accurately at a target as small as a song-
bird up to five hundred metres away, if the scopes can pick it
up unobstructed.

Sawyer attempts to hand out the guns, but none of the
bumpkins will take one. They look at the shoeboxes like there
are stink bombs inside, like they're a child's prank.

"I'll stick with my M82," one cousin says.

"Can't hit a barn with that." But Sawyer knows they never
had a gun that big. They force one into Obsidian's hands, un-
fold their own and strap it over their shoulder.

Aiden sneers at them from the back seat of his mother's
Benz. Sawyer resists the urge to get him in their scope, just
to make him shit his pants. It wouldn't go over well with his
father, though his mother might laugh it off.

Sawyer, the first on the speakers list, keeps their promise to
introduce their father without much editorial. They shout into

the bullhorn (unnecessarily, they realize, but once they've started shouting it seems weird to stop, so they keep at it): "I'd like
to introduce my father! A great, great man who has sacrificed
whatever it takes for you true farmers. Not just for you, but for
all of us. For the sake of food, and our need to eat it!" It feels so
stupid shouting this and Sawyer will for sure add themselves to
their stupids list. But it's important they all hear this, all sides:
the cousins, the vagrants, and the true farmers.

A metallic thunder claps the not-so-distant section of Route
1 asphalt, and supplicant engines roar. Obsidian's knee seizes
as he makes the slight ascent over the edge of the stage and
stumbles forward. He wears a plaid shirt and a floppy straw
hat, like a Halloween costume of a farmer. He's a work of art.

LANDON

Only going for you, little Cranky Girl, as always I go for you,
getting so tired but that's what a daddy does for his little
Cranky Girl. Don't mind her, she threw her strained peas all
over me and her mom but she's just a little cranky girl. And
she don't know what to do with me. Can't blame her for that. I
don't know what to do with me either, anymore.

Used to have plenty to do, used to manage the biggest retail
operation east of Montreal for many fine years of which I can
be most proud. Bet I could still find my way to that store, if
my son-in-law would let me off his leash. They tell me it's not
there anymore, which if true is a deeply depressing, shameful
thing. It's a wonderful place, with five entire rows of diverse
produce, four of which contain fresh fruits and vegetables
flown in double time from all over the world, and the other of

which is all local goods as tops as at any farmers' market in the province. That's not even going into all the merchandise, the clothing and electronics and appliances. The place they shop now, to which they take me every single time because they say I need to get off my screens and stop watching the silver joys of my childhood ... I forget where I was going with that.

Anyway, I have seen endless canned goods towering over my head, I have dreamed of them cascading down upon me like blows from a battalion at close range. They crack open before I do and all that comes out is a singular beige slime, the same thing they feed me thrice daily, which they say is the thing that keeps me alive until tomorrow. I don't want to die, but I must, in time, before much more. Going to these stores is something to do anyway, until then.

Only going for you, dear Cranky Girl. You were my world all my life. I raised you with books and I told you to be whatever you wanted, and sometimes you even smiled and you always made me proud of your degrees and prizes and well-paid positions. You were the first to notice my confusion and you and your husband, whatshisname, take me — he takes me to the library and that's something to do, anyway. Somewhere to be.

Today there are tractors lined across the highway and we stop on the way and my dear Cranky Girl buys me something delicious over whatshisname's protests that it's overpriced heart-attack food. "It will keep him busy, anyway," you say. You give him the paper bowl and take my hands with your soft palms, mould them into a cup for holding. Whatshisname concedes and gives me the paper bowl, which is filled with that food I used to love, it's called ... it's little strips of that root vegetable, that one we're known for. Little strips of golden-brown, with flecks of salt. In a bowl made of newspaper with a headline sticking out that says "Dehydrated hedgehogs: Heat wave takes toll."

There's a piece of wood jammed in one of the little potato strips. It's like a pitchfork, only tiny, for picking up the things to eat. The bowl is warm in my hands and I can't figure it out, Cranky Girl, how to get my fingers on the pitchfork without dropping the whole contraption. So I hold it careful and steady as we drive past a few tractors, Little Cranky, you tooting the horn, which sings some old familiar pop song, a happy-sounding one about being sad. I lean in with my mouth and take a bite. It's hot but so incredible I shout while I chew: "It fills me with a precious essence, or rather the essence is me!"

"Don't talk while you chew," Whatshisname says.

I swallow but don't apologize to your whatshisname, who is crankier than you sometimes. We arrive at the scene, all the farmers with their tractors lined across the highway. Something to do, I suppose. Some place to be.

"My grandfather," I say, but I forgot I had filled my mouth with more ecstasy, and in the instant I move my mouth I am a child lying in sunshine on red sand, salt on my lips, waves and seagulls harmonizing for me. Why didn't you tell me your world had this feeling in it? How can you be cranky with this available any time you want it?

I'm teasing you — you know that, right? You aren't always cranky.

My grandfather, Donald Arsenault he was called, he used to own this spot, before the bridge or the highway. He had a corner store here. I've told you this story. It burned with all his stock, crowded counters to the tin ceiling filled with bolts of cloth and coils of rope and tins of paint and plenty of jarred cabbage, and apples and molasses and sweets for the kids, jawbreakers and licorice whips, which he kept on the top shelves and we would have to ask him to hoist us up to get any, which he did by the hips with a gleeful laugh, shouting, "Hurry hurry I have work to do!" but he'd hold us until we found what we wanted. He only pretended to be cranky. He survived the fire, but his spirit was broken.

The speeches are starting and I wander about, something to do, and I've got my snack small enough I can hold it with one hand and use the little wooden pitchfork with the other, feeding myself morsels of svelte savoury. I know the young lady speaking; she's coming down now from the little black stage, which they set up right on the road. What's her name again? She's got beautiful musculature, must be strong, maybe a gymnast, or a biathlete. She's got her gun over her shoulder, black and smooth and quite large. Can people still ski?

I approach her and she snarls, another cranky girl, Cranky Girl. A cranky young lady. I smile and offer her a bite and it hits me. "They're called fries, dear. You should try one. Fresh. I couldn't remember what they were called at first, because there's no label. You know better when you have a label."

"Yes, you know better what it's supposed to be when you have a label," she says. "But when you eat it, you can't tell if you're alive or dead. Can you?"

She's so smart, but I fear for that young lady. You had the same problem when you were young, Cranky Girl. Still I can't disagree. "It's just something to do."

THE CRANE

Jacqueline Valencia

hese days it seems like every moment, something life changing will happen. I mean, it's always felt like this to me, since I was little. I remember the first time I thought about death. It was my fourth birthday and my parents had invited family over to share a meal and cake, over music on a Saturday night. Colombians find any excuse to make a family get-together.

My aunts and uncles were talking about someone who died recently in the family that was still in Cali. I asked my mother what *muerte* meant. She said it's when someone goes to heaven. I knew what heaven was, but I quickly realized that meant everyone was going to leave! If everyone died, then I would be left alone one day. As someone who knew nothing but school and her parents, the first thing that came to mind after that was "Who is going to feed me?"

It was ridiculous, though, I was four, but my mother's cooking and my family's cooking is what I lived for as a child. Big breakfasts of buñuelos (round cheese pastries), pericos (scrambled eggs with tomatoes and green onions), served with beans, and a bowl — yes, a bowl — of hot chocolate. As an adult, I don't really indulge in those big breakfasts anymore, but occasionally I'll make myself components of them, as a treat. So now I know the answer is that a single man can feed himself, and occasionally I get the chance to feed others.

Nowadays, I go for walks along the lakeshore in the early morning. I worry, not just about people leaving, but the endless what-ifs in my day. What if I fall down and hit my head and forget where I live? Who will feed my cats? How will they know they're in my apartment alone? This is why I carry a pet information card. What if the ATM goes down before I do groceries? This is why I have cash in a hidden place. What if I need to stay inside again for a month or so, due to a pandemic or nuclear event? This is why I have a survival kit in my storage locker.

I could go on.

My walks take me to a nice view of the Port Lands. It's an area of Toronto that is constantly under construction, under demolishment, changing, or under consideration. A couple of new white-and-red bridges have appeared among the factory and construction sand dunes that frame the 215-metre-tall smokestack of the Hearn Generating Station. The stack doesn't do anything, but it's a sight before dawn as the light at the top blinks to prevent planes from hitting it.

My mind often wanders and looks for something to get anxious about. The sights by the lake give me pause from the panic. The smokestack is huge and if I were standing in front of it, it would surely fall because who would see that coming? Me, that's who. So I found myself looking at the Port Lands on the horizon and wondering about something else besides the stack.

To the far left of the imposing stack is the giant three-hundred-tonne Atlas crane. It's not as startling to me as the stack, but it is a charming eyeful from afar. From where I stand, looking at it, the crane has four branches that look like really long legs, and meet up at a bridge-like connection on the top. The joints and, most likely, the places where the mechanics and construction crews manoeuvred it look like big hats on either end of it. Other joints in the middle of the branches look like garter belts, for decor. With the sunlight hitting the back of the crane, the whole of it looks as if it were conjoined twins wearing top hats and garters, ready to tap dance their way out into the lake. "Hello my baby, hello my honey ..." always pops up in my head when I look at it.

———

Twilight before dawn and my anxiety is laying a foundation of wandering thoughts. Have I paid my rent? I know I have, because I screencapped the landlord's withdrawal in my bank app. Have I fed the cats? Yes, I did, because I am looking at the photo I took of the cats eating. My phone is full of photos like this.

———

A big star that seems to be always by the crane twinkles, and that is when my brain goes from cats to what if the crane is struck by lightning? What if it came to life? Would it need to eat? If it ate, what would it eat?

———

I'm really not bringing this up out of nowhere. That morning I read an article about scientists creating a magnetic slime robot that could pull things out of your body. I'm sure that thing needs fuel. Everything mechanical needs fuel, and in this day and age I've been learning that anything can happen. If the crane is struck by lightning and suddenly needs to feed to dance, what would it eat? I suspect that, after unloading the ships that contained food, streetcars, and all sorts of things that the city needs from the world, it would be hungry. It spent many long years sitting there after being decommissioned. Would its heads look around at the dirt and the water and attempt to eat what was in front of it? It only has sand dunes around it and the empty structures that it most likely helped build.

I know. I know. It would most likely need gasoline, but if we're talking about anything happening when it's been struck by lightning, maybe it would have a choice of foods to try. The crane would stomp over to the first dune, pick up a bunch of gravel and sand with its scoop, and feed it to one of its heads. Then it would cough because sand and gravel are dry. Crane would then try to mix the sand with dirt and it would make a big mess of itself. Hilarious.

"Toronto! I am alive now. How do I eat?"

It would then try to munch on the bricks of the Cherry Street Bar-B-Que or the Keating Channel Pub. Finding it palatable, Crane would sit by the channel and put off contemplating its new-found existence as it discovered sustenance and a means to continue. Suddenly being able to move and do something after just sitting there, seeing the city grow and go on without it, Crane would have a lot to contemplate.

But what if bricks weren't enough? It would be very fortunate if bricks, mortar, and cement were what Crane needed to survive, since Toronto is full of all those things and maybe too much of them. Life doesn't work if it's easy and convenient — at least, that's what I've learned. There aren't too many what-ifs in an easy life and how does one live without worry? I don't know.

It would be great if Crane could survive only if it ate humans. While there are many of us, we are quickly creating a place where there will be fewer of us, making life harder for Crane. You see, there'd be a point where Crane finds someone screaming at this walking monster and Crane would reach out with its scoop to say hello. It would proceed to accidentally crush and consume a man on his way to work and the man would be delicious. He'd taste like expensive Harbour 60 steak, the one you can cut with a butter knife. Rawr. Rawr. Rawr. Bloodthirsty Crane versus the world.

Out of my head and into reality, a plane passes the stack and the crane toward the airport. Ducks and geese have gathered beside me on the water, looking expectantly at me. I pull some birdseed from my pocket and throw it their way. I walk farther from them to avoid the eventual seagulls and check the weather. No sign of rain today. I think about the other things happening on Earth at the moment: the wars, violence, injustice, illness, and death. Gazing at the three-hundred-tonne Atlas crane, I worry about the rain that will come eventually and whether I'll still be alive that day. Anything can happen. If I'm here and Crane comes alive, will it eat me? What if us humans aren't here — who's going to feed my cats? What is going to happen to Crane?

The sun is fully up and I walk away from the lake while adding more worries to the list. Hot chocolate waits to be made at home.

RECIPE FROM THE FUTURE

Gary Barwin

I n the future, we'll eat the future. It's pretty tasty. Not like the past. Or pasta. In the future, that joke will be funny. We don't eat the present. There's nothing so unsavoury or unsavioury as the present. Except maybe my shorts. Though with a good white sauce and a glass of rosé, they could make a decent meal in a pinch. Or in a future where all forms of agriculture are gone. In the future, we'll eat their words. Plus, the burning sky and the lakes, which are even more acidic than they used to be. Like apple pie. Which also isn't like it used to be. Or like it's going to be. You know what I miss? Sadness. Know what we call that now? Lunch.

My love, Mary, knocked on the door. Okay, knocked on a tree. There were no doors anymore. Also, no trees. She just walked near me and said, "Knock knock." I bet you're expecting a joke now. Who's there? It was Mary. I ate all the knock-knock jokes years ago. I was hungry. And desperate. There's still some "A Catholic, a reclining chair, and a diaper walk into a bar" jokes. Thank God. We need something, Mary and me. All of us. Maybe we are all there is. I haven't seen anyone except us for a long time. Really, she got up from her haunches around the fire, walked a little bit away, and then turned around and said, "Knock knock." What you gonna do? We gotta do something to maintain the illusion of civilization. I mean, now that it's gone.

Hey, Tom, Mary said. A guy walks up to God and tells him a joke about the future. God says, That's not funny. I guess you had to be there, the guy says.

Oh ho, I said to Mary. That's a zinger. That's a good joke. What's for lunch?

Don't ask me, Mary said. I'm just a guest.

Okay, we could eat our hopes and dreams.

And sorrows, Mary said.

We have lots of them, I said.

What happened to our baby? she asked.

I wiped my mouth and looked guilty.

Oh no, Mary said. You didn't go all "A Modest Proposal" on me?

No, no. I didn't eat the baby. I let the baby grow up.

Oh good, Mary said.

It's a form of agriculture, I said.

Mary gasped again.

Just joking. Guess you had to be there.

I was, she said.

Ergo, you're not God.

Right. But where's the baby?

Foraging.

Foraging?

Among the weeds and the rusty deeds of civilization.
Seeking entrails amid the flames.

Seems a fool's game.

It is. Though I remember once, I must have been a child
then, when I found a chicken.

A chicken?

Well, not so much of a chicken as a rat. But ...

You're not going to tell me that it tasted like chicken?

It was more the memory of chicken. Or the memory the old
folks used to share when we hid underground.

———

Mary sat back down on her haunches and we tucked rags under
our chins because we were getting ready for lunch. I hope you
realize that this story I'm telling you is made up. Things weren't
so bad. We had fire. We had a future, which we could hope to
eat. In which we could hope to eat. The moon came out big in
the dirty sky above us and Mary and me made love on the dirty
ground. We had parts. They fit together. We had love. We had
hope. The future was like a rusted-out car and the weeds grew
around it. It had its own story. We loved it. It fascinated us and
it was a place where we could seek shelter and comfort. Even
in a storm. Of rain or snow. Not that there was snow anymore.
But okay, this is a story. We had our little lunches that Mother
packed. Sometime, a long time ago in the past, Mother packed
us lunches. Sandwiches. A pickle. Juice. Here, Tom and Mary,
this is for the future. You're going to need to eat in the future.
It's going to be a hungry time and you can't live on hope and
love alone. You'll need lunch.

If there was a God in the future, that God would be like a sandwich. Or, to be more specific, that God would be like bread and we'd be the peanut butter and jam. God like two soft and cushy slices making us into something. Otherwise, we'd just be smears, smudges, not any kind of lunch at all. Though we'd be pressed together. Both of us, under the big moon, peanut butter and jam, two knifefuls in the future, always hoping for bread.

Bread, Mary said. Were you talking about bread?

Guess I was thinking out loud, I said. Sometimes hunger is so big it floods the banks of the brain and comes out talking. Prayers. Stories. How could a brain keep it all in?

I remember when our baby was small and we were two slices of bread on either side of him, keeping him safe and warm.

He was our peanut butter.

Our jelly.

Eventually it was morning. It looked a lot like the night before, except we couldn't see the moon. Or we couldn't imagine it. We had to imagine the sun behind the pearly gate of cloud. The sun, way out there somewhere, cooking us like hams.

Mary, I said. But there was no answer. Mary, I said louder, more like a yell. *Mary!* But I heard only the echo of my own voice. Well, I didn't even hear the echo. There was nothing but emptiness for it to echo off. Maybe I was yelling inside my own head and the echo that I heard was the echo of nothingness, of my own thoughts making nothing happen in the world, not

even bringing our baby back to our home around the fire. There
was no fire. Were there ashes? There were no ashes. Maybe
there'd never been ashes. Maybe I ate them. Fire and ashes
sandwich. A sandwich made out of my own voice. Wasn't there
something about a sentence being a sandwich? Was a paragraph
a hamburger? I remember talking about a knuckle sandwich.
Nothing to eat but pain.

———————

The future won't be the same as this future. Or it'll be the same
but even more so. Big rock candy future with streams filled
with sandwich meat. I remember once Mary and I cooked a
rabbit. Maybe it was a squirrel. We had a fire and a stick and
Mary put the squirrel on the stick and I held it over the fire.
The sound was like electric sizzling. From back when there was
electricity. You know what Mary was? She was an archeologist.
She'd dig things up and tell me about them. And I was a his-
torian. I'd remember what she said.

Let's be our own institute, I said.

Yes, she said. I'll be the president.

Okay, I said. Can I be chair of the board and I'll give you a
headache because I'll suggest things that aren't helpful?

Right, Mary said. We'll have a gala.

Yes, I said. We'll have finger food.

Perfect, Mary said. And tiny little sausages and cheese.

I'd love that, I said. And those little sticks with frizzy col-
oured plastic on the end.

Great, Mary said.

And some shaped like tiny swords.

Drinks with umbrellas! I said.

Oh yes! Mary said.

Yes, yes, yes, yes, yes.

———————

I'm sitting in a chair in my dining room and there's no one here. Except me, of course. Mary's at work. She's an archeologist. That means she studies the past. She's hungry for the past. And she has a spade. A big one and a little one. She sits on her haunches and looks for old things. If the present were mashed potatoes and you dug into it, there'd be more mashed potatoes. The past is the present, just not yet. The future is different, though. There's no mashed potatoes in the future.

Mary, I said. I'm really worried.

Worried? What worries you?

The future, Mary. I'm scared.

Me too, Mary said.

Really?

Of course, Mary said. That's why I'm studying the past.

So you can learn from it?

So I don't have to learn from the future.

———————

Once I had a theory. The past was a slice of bread. The future was a slice of bread. The present was nestled safely in between like peanut butter and jelly. Time and our lives were a sandwich. I don't believe that theory anymore. Is time an open-faced sandwich? No. The future isn't missing — there just isn't any bread there. Or mashed potatoes. When we get there, all we'll be able to do is eat the future. It's a bad cloud and our bellies are bad clouds. Bad clouds inside bad clouds.

———————

I'm here at our dining table and I'm thinking about the future.

Knock knock. The future. Who's there? You're too late.

I'm at our dining table and I'm writing a recipe book. I'm calling it *Recipes for the Future*. All the ingredients are things from the past so when you get to the future, you won't be able to make any of the recipes. Except for one. It was Mary's idea.

You have an idea for a recipe that we'll be able to eat in the future?

Yes, Mary said. Here's the recipe: take the book *Recipes for the Future*, and eat it.

That's good, I said. Really good.

Yes, she said. And what's especially good is that people will have to buy lots of copies of the book if they are to survive.

Oh, I want to go with you into the future, I said. And not because I want you for lunch.

No?

Well, okay, I said and removed my shorts. There, right on the dining table, we made love as if we were a recipe from the future. It wasn't anything like chicken. Not even the memory of chicken. The moon was in the big sky or the sun was in the big sky and we were on the big dining-room table and we began the process of making a baby, a baby that would grow quick as corn but be less like a meal. I imagined our baby not able to walk or even to sit up, so it'd be lying down. It'd be horizontal with its head in the kitchen and its feet in the hall, if the kitchen was the past and the hall was the future. The present would be somewhere around its belly and we'd fill its belly with lots of good things, like peanut butter and jelly sandwiches or chicken.

———

This is a story, but who knows how it's going to end. Sometime soon, we're going to get to the end and then it'll be over. Oh, Mary and me, we'll have our memories. We'll sit on our haunches by the fire, we'll hold hands by the fire and remember. We'll tell the story from the beginning and then when we get to the end, we'll start all over again. We'll tell our story from the kitchen to the hall, from its head to its toes, our baby, sweet as apple pie. And the future, the future will be like a big ol' apple pie too, except an apple pie with no apples and no crust, either. All there'll be will be the future. The future waiting for us to eat it. The future that's run out of past and that's run out of present. The future that doesn't taste like chicken and that doesn't taste like apple pie. That's good because I'd like a future that doesn't taste like chicken and doesn't taste like apple pie. Oh, sorry, sir, we're all out of chicken and we're all out of apple pie. Could you have a future without white sauce and without rosé? Oh, I could have a future without them, I just couldn't have a future without Mary. Mary, I shouted. Mary, I'm hungry and I'm waiting for you here in the future, here in the future by the fire, the future that isn't the end of the story but something more like lunch.

EDITORS

Jeff Dupuis is a writer, editor, and podcaster based in Toronto. He is the co-founder of *The Quarantine Review* and the author of three novels. His most recent book, *Umboi Island*, was released in March of 2022 by Dundurn Press.

A.G. Pasquella's writing has appeared in various spots, including *McSweeney's*, *Wholphin*, *The Believer*, *Black Book*, *Broken Pencil*, and *Little Brother*. He was the co-editor (along with Terri Favro) of *Pac'n Heat: A Noir Homage to Ms. Pac-Man*. Pasquella's novellas — *Why Not a Spider Monkey Jesus?* (which also appeared as a thirty-page excerpt in *McSweeney's* #11), *NewTown*, and *The This & the That* — were republished by Wolsak & Wynn in an omnibus titled *Welcome to the Weird America*. Pasquella's three crime thrillers in the Jack Palace Series — *Yard Dog*, *Carve the Heart*, and *Season of Smoke* — were published by Dundurn Press.

CONTRIBUTORS

Sifton Tracey Anipare was born in Windsor, Ontario, to Ghanaian parents. A writer, dancer, cinephile, gamer, and musician since childhood, she has always been fascinated by strange stories. She completed an honours bachelor of science at the University of Toronto and an internship with the Toronto International Film Festival before pursuing an education career that began with the JET Programme in Japan. When she is not writing, she will rewatch her favourite movies or play video games for hours on end. Her first full-length novel, *Yume*, was published in September 2021; it has since garnered praise for its otherworldly take on inequality and self-actualization in a dark fantasy world.

Carleigh Baker is an author and teacher of nêhiyaw âpiht-awikosisân and European descent. Born and raised on Stó:lō territory, she currently lives on the unceded territories of the xʷməθkʷəy̓əm, S̲k̲w̲x̲wú7mesh, and səl̓ilwəta peoples. Her debut story collection, *Bad Endings* (Anvil Press, 2017), won the City of Vancouver Book Award, and was also a finalist for the Rogers Writers' Trust Fiction Prize and the Emerging Indigenous Voices Award for fiction. Her newest collection, *Last Woman*, and a novel are forthcoming with McClelland & Stewart. As a teacher and researcher, she is particularly interested in how contemporary fiction can be used to address the climate crisis.

Gary Barwin is a writer, performer, multimedia artist, and the author of twenty-nine books, including *Nothing the Same, Everything Haunted: The Ballad of Motl the Cowboy*, which won the Canadian Jewish Literary Award, and *The Most Charming Creatures*, his most recent poetry collection. His national bestselling novel, *Yiddish for Pirates*, won the Leacock Medal for Humour and the Canadian Jewish Literary Award, was a finalist for the Governor General's Award for fiction and the Scotiabank Giller Prize, and was longlisted for Canada Reads. He currently lives in Hamilton, Ontario, and at garybarwin.com.

Chris Benjamin is the author of five books. His latest is a travel memoir, *Chasing Paradise: A Hitchhiker's Search for Home in a World at War with Itself*, about hitchhiking around North America before and after 9/11. His short story collection, *Boy with a Problem*, was shortlisted for the Alistair MacLeod Prize for Short Fiction. His book *Eco-Innovators: Sustainability in Atlantic Canada* was shortlisted for the Evelyn Richardson Non-Fiction Award and won the Best Atlantic-Published Book Award. He works as part of the Energy & Climate team at the Ecology Action Centre in Halifax, where he lives with his wife, children, and Mookie the Burping Dog.

Eddy Boudel Tan is the author of two novels: *After Elias* (Dundurn Press), a finalist for the Edmund White Award and the ReLit Award, and *The Rebellious Tide* (Dundurn Press), a finalist for the Ferro-Grumley Award. In 2021, he was named a Rising Star by the Writers' Trust of Canada. His short stories can be found in *Joyland, Yolk, Gertrude Press,* and *The G&LR,* as well as the anthologies *Queer Little Nightmares* (Arsenal Pulp Press) and *The Spirits Have Nothing to Do with Us* (Wolsak & Wynn). He lives in Vancouver with his husband, where he's writing his next novel while deciphering the language of birds.

Catherine Bush is the author of five novels, including *Blaze Island* (2020), a *Globe & Mail* Best Book and the Hamilton Reads 2021 selection; and *The Rules of Engagement* (2000), a national bestseller and *New York Times* Notable Book. Her books, which have been shortlisted for the Trillium and Toronto Book Awards, among others, often explore intersections of realism and the speculative. Her non-fiction has been published in the *New York Times, Brick, Emergence, Noema,* and *Best Canadian Essays.* She teaches creative writing at the University of Guelph and lives in Toronto. She can be found online at catherinebush.com.

Jowita Bydlowska is a writer whose last novel, *Possessed,* was considered "too explicit" in Canada.

Lisa de Nikolits has been hailed as "the Queen of Canadian speculative fiction" (All Lit Up) and is the international award-winning author of eleven novels. Her short fiction and poetry have been published in various international anthologies and journals. Lisa's work has appeared on recommended reading lists for both Open Book Toronto and the 49th Shelf, and has been chosen as a *Chatelaine* Editor's Pick and a *Canadian Living* Magazine Must-Read. Her novel *The Occult Persuasion and the Anarchist's Solution* was longlisted for a Sunburst Award for Excellence in Canadian Literature of the Fantastic. Her most recent book, *The Rage Room*, was a finalist in the International Book Awards. She has lived in Canada since 2000. She has a bachelor of arts in English literature and philosophy and has lived in the U.S., Australia, and Britain. lisawriter.com.

Dina Del Bucchia is the author of the short story collection *Don't Tell Me What to Do* and four collections of poetry: *Coping with Emotions and Otters*, *Blind Items*, *Rom Com* (written with Daniel Zomparelli), and *It's a Big Deal!* She also started the podcast *Can't Lit* with Daniel and now hosts with Jen Sookfong Lee. She is the artistic director of the Real Vancouver Writers' Series, on the editorial board of fine. press, and writes the newsletter *Hey Fuckface*. An otter and dress enthusiast, she lives in Vancouver. You can find out more about her at dinadelbucchia.com or follow her, @DelBauchery, on X or Instagram.

Terri Favro is a novelist, essayist, and storyteller who loves writing about migration, comic strips, superheroes, robots, and weird science. Her most recent book is *The Sisters Sputnik*, sequel to *Sputnik's Children* (a *Globe* 100 book, longlisted for Canada Reads). She's also the author of the popular science book *Generation Robot: A Century of Science Fiction, Fact, and Speculation*. Terri lives in Toronto, where she collaborates on graphic novels with her visual artist husband and eagerly awaits the event horizon of the Singularity, when humans and machines merge, hallelujah! Check out her blog at terrifavro.ca.

Elan Mastai is a novelist and screenwriter. His award-winning debut novel, *All Our Wrong Todays*, was published by Penguin Random House and translated into two dozen languages. In 2021, he was nominated for an Emmy Award for his work on the hit TV series *This Is Us*, where he spent three seasons as a writer and rose to co-executive producer of the show's sixth and final season. He won the Canadian Academy Award and the Writers Guild of Canada award for his screenplay for the movie *The F Word* — released as *What If* in the U.S. — starring Daniel Radcliffe, Zoe Kazan, Adam Driver, and Mackenzie Davis, which premiered at the Toronto International Film Festival.

Mark Sampson has published four novels: *All the Animals on Earth* (Wolsak & Wynn, 2020), *The Slip* (Dundurn Press, 2017), *Sad Peninsula* (Dundurn Press, 2014), and *Off Book* (Norwood Publishing, 2007). He has also published a short story collection, *The Secrets Men Keep* (Now or Never Publishing, 2015), and a poetry collection, *Weathervane* (Palimpsest Press, 2016). Born and raised on Prince Edward Island, he currently lives and writes in Toronto.

Ji Hong Sayo is a Canadian-Lao-Chinese author working out of Toronto. His first book was the science fiction novel *Rise*, published while he was attending high school in New Delhi, India. He loves writing about clever, fearless, just-slightly-evil characters, and weaving a thread of romance through action-focused genres. By day, Ji studies biomedical engineering at the University of Toronto, where he has also worked as a researcher. Biology being his specialty, his writing often features a rare poison or a mysterious mutation. When he isn't writing, Ji can be found training at the Central Toronto Wrestling Club, cooking for his family, or playing tag with his little brother and cousins.

Jacqueline Valencia is a Toronto-based writer, essayist, and activist. She is the author of various essays and poetry books, including *There Is No Escape Out of Time* (Insomniac Press, 2016) and *Lilith* (Desert Pets Press, 2018). She is a project partner at Poetry inPrint, founding editor of the online film magazine *Critical Focus*, and organizer for the 2015 Poetry Talks: Racism and Sexism in the Craft. Jacqueline is a member of the Meet the Presses collective and an editor at Many Gendered Mothers. You can find her at jacquelinevalencia.ca.

Anuja Varghese is a Pushcart-nominated QWOC writer based in Hamilton, Ontario. Her work appears in *The Malahat Review*, *Hobart*, *The Fiddlehead*, and *Plenitude Magazine*, as well as the *Queer Little Nightmares* anthology (Arsenal Pulp Press, 2022), among others. Anuja serves as fiction editor for *The Ex-Puritan* magazine, as well as a board member for gritLIT, Hamilton's literary festival, and host of LitLive, Hamilton's monthly reading series. Anuja holds a degree in English literature from McGill University and is currently pursuing a Creative Writing Certificate from the University of Toronto, while working on a debut novel. Her short story collection, *Chrysalis* (House of Anansi Press, 2023), explores South Asian diaspora experience through a feminist, speculative lens. She can be found on Instagram, X, and TikTok (@anuja_v across platforms), or by visiting her website, anujavarghese.com.

A.G.A. Wilmot is a writer, editor, and painter based out of Toronto, Ontario. They have won awards for fiction, short fiction, and screenwriting — including the Friends of the Merril Short Story Contest and ECW Press's Best New Speculative Novel Contest — and are co-publisher and co-editor-in-chief of the Ignyte Award– and British Fantasy Award–nominated *Anathema: Spec from the Margins*. Their credits include myriad online and in-print publications and anthologies. They are also on the editorial advisory board for Poplar Press, the speculative fiction imprint of Wolsak & Wynn. Other books of A.G.A.'s include *The Death Scene Artist* (Buckrider Books, 2018) and *Withered* (ECW Press, 2024). They are represented by Kelvin Kong of K2 Literary. Find them online at agawilmot.ca.